Catching
Cooper

Catching
Cooper
A Red Maple Falls Novel

Happy Reading!

Theresa Paolo

Theresa Paolo

Dedicated to Eric
who always tells me to order the damn dessert

Red *Maple* Falls

A small town with big personalities

Chapter 1

Cooper Hayes was bored. The itch inside him to take off was craving its next adventure. It was like this invisible rope, relentlessly tugging and refusing to leave him alone.

He had travelled to seventy-four countries over the past seven years, chronicling his experiences and becoming a popular travel blogger and social media sensation. But he had grown tired of the constant on-the-go and being away from his family, so he'd come back home to the small town of Red Maple Falls.

But being home was a reminder of why he'd left. His days were monotonous, and while he loved kayaking with his oldest brother, Matt, and helping his other brother and best friend, Mason get his brewery up and running, after almost nine months he couldn't ignore the itch. Which was why he volunteered to man the cash register at his very pregnant sister-in-law's bakery while she was home on doctor ordered bedrest—he was desperate to occupy his mind. Even wrote a book after Mason suggested it, putting his travels and experiences onto paper. Even bigger, he managed to snag an agent within a couple months of querying. But now that he had finished the book and was waiting on editors at publishing houses to get back to his agent, he was growing restless again.

The pull to find his next big venture was strong, but he couldn't leave now. Not when his big brother was about to become a dad. He wanted to meet the little guy who would be arriving any day now. At least they all hoped so; Shay was going to snap, and they'd be dealing with his brother's murder instead of the birth of Cooper's nephew.

Shay looked like she was smuggling a beach ball beneath her shirt and was growing impatient while Matt was losing his mind with worry. His constant freak outs were driving his poor wife insane. While it was entertaining, it still wasn't enough to scratch the itch and that made Cooper feel guilty.

Red Maple Falls, the town he was born and raised and absolutely loved wasn't enough. His family wasn't enough. No matter how many people he met, how many ruins he explored, he was always looking toward what was next. He was looking for the thing that made him feel complete.

The bell above the bakery door chimed, and Cooper pushed off the counter, plastering on his famous smile—the same smile that got him out of countless predicaments and scored him free room and board across the world.

"How can I help you today?" he asked as two perfect onyx stones caught his own eyes. Her lip tilted slightly as she approached the counter, long black hair in waves bouncing on her shoulders. Cooper always had a high appreciation of the opposite sex, and this woman was no exception.

She pointed a long finger at the display case. He noted the lack of nail polish which made him think either she couldn't be bothered with the glitz and glam or she simply didn't have the time. She also wasn't wearing a ring, which, in his eyes, signified an invitation to flirt.

"I'll take a blueberry muffin," she said without hesitation.

"A woman who knows what she wants," he said, and her eyebrow arched but not in the way he'd hoped. She looked at him with disdain, like he was a joke, and she was waiting for the punch-line. He was usually quick-witted, but he suddenly forgot how to form complete sentences.

"You know... You want..." He mentally smacked himself for losing his cool. He'd seen millions of women around the world, bedded too many to remember, yet this woman with her sinfully dark eyes and silky long hair who barely gave him a second glance had him tongue-tied. He smiled at his idiocy then took a deep breath and tried again. "Most people come in here and take an hour to decide. You knew exactly what you wanted without even glancing at any of the other pastries or cupcakes."

"I come here every Monday, and every Monday I get the blueberry muffin. To go, please."

"Coming right up." He grabbed one of the light pink paper bags with the bakery logo—a cupcake with a hot pink and black striped baking cup and Sweet Dreams Bakery written in girly font above—and placed the muffin inside. He slid it across the counter to her, and she already had the exact amount due in her hand.

"Why Monday?" he asked as he entered the information into the cash register as slowly as he could.

"It's my treat for getting through another week."

He took the money, pausing as their fingers touched. "Why not Friday, then?"

"A week consists of seven days," she said matter-of-factly. "Wouldn't want to celebrate prematurely."

"Yes, but the weekend is for relaxing and having fun. You look like you could use a little fun."

He smiled, but she didn't. He imagined his hand would turn to ice if he touched her face right now.

"Some people don't get days off."

"That's no way to live."

"I don't remember paying extra for your opinion." There was venom in her tone, but that never deterred Cooper before.

He held his hands up in mock surrender. "Sorry. What I was trying to say, and failing miserably at, is I'd love to take you out sometime. Show you there's nothing wrong with a little fun."

He waited for the flutter of eyelashes, the slight blush filling her cheeks that all the girls got when he asked them out, but it never came. "No thanks."

Taken aback, he didn't hide his shock. "Wow, you don't beat around the bush."

Her gaze lifted to his, the two dark stones showing no sign of emotion. "Why would I do that?"

"Because it can soften the blow."

"I prefer to rip the Band-aid off. No reason to drag it out."

"I can appreciate that approach."

Her eyebrow lifted in what he could only assume was doubt. "Can you?"

No matter what he did, she wouldn't even give him an inch. "I feel like we should start over."

"Why?"

"Because I'm getting the feeling you don't like me based on preconceived notions. If you look beyond my devilish good looks and charming personality, I'm not a bad guy."

"I think you've given me plenty to base my opinion on."

"Ouch." This woman was insufferable and somehow immune to his charm. He pulled out all the stops and not a single smile. To say he was intrigued would be the understatement of the century.

She took a deep breath and let it out slowly, her stoic expression softening. "I'm sorry. I'm being rude."

"Hey, you said it."

"I can admit when I'm in the wrong. I just can't have dinner with you. I'm sorry."

"Can't or won't?"

"Maybe a little of both." Her voice softened, and he could detect the faintest touch of sorrow.

"Because you don't have time for fun?"

"Something like that."

"Well, I'll keep the invitation open. If you ever find the time, let me know."

"It's unlikely."

"We need to work on your sugarcoating. Don't say 'unlikely.' Say, 'we'll see.'"

"Okay then. We'll see." She smiled, and the slight curve of her lips brightened up her entire face, transforming her into an entirely different person—someone who looked warm and friendly, who would jump on the chance for a good time.

He handed her the receipt, figuring he'd stalled long enough. "I'm Cooper by the way. Shay's world travelling brother-in-law."

"The one who showed up late to the wedding?"

He laughed. "The one who wasn't even going to make the wedding but flew halfway across the world and made everyone cry by showing up."

"Do you always like to steal people's thunder?"

"You go straight for the jugular."

She shrugged. "How is Shay doing?"

"Good, but I'm more concerned about my brother's

health. I think if he doesn't lay off a little, she's going to cause physical harm, and I can't say I blame her."

"At least she has someone who cares that much about her. She's lucky."

"I'm sure she'll realize that one day. After she pops the kid out and her ankles don't look like tree stumps anymore."

"Please don't say that to her."

"Are you crazy? I like everything intact, thank you very much. Besides one wrong word and she's either seething or crying."

"Pregnancy hormones are no joke."

"Apparently."

"When you do see her, tell her I asked about her."

"I could do that, but I would need to know your name."

"Sarah Kramer."

"Well, Sarah Kramer, it has been a pleasure. Although, I'm pretty sure you insulted me more than once."

"More than once," she said, that rare smile showing up and spreading wider than before.

"I really hope you find time in your busy schedule to let me take you to dinner. I can guarantee you won't regret it."

"See, that's where you're wrong." She didn't elaborate, just took her bag with the blueberry muffin and walked out the door without as much a glance back in his direction.

***

Cooper pulled up to Matt and Shay's house and grabbed the pastry box filled with a variety of the current offerings at the bakery. As he was about to head to the front door, he spotted his brother out on the deck overlooking the lake, so Cooper detoured.

"Hey," he said as he walked up the steps, noticing the

beer in his brother's hand. His fingers were wrapped around the bottle tightly, his knuckles practically white. If he held on any tighter, the bottle would shatter into a million pieces just like Matt's patience. The thought made Cooper laugh.

"What are you laughing at?" Matt asked as he took a swig from the bottle.

"Did Shay put you in time out?"

Matt's lip curled. "I just asked her if she needed anything, and she told me if I didn't leave her alone she would give me something to worry about."

Cooper stifled a laugh the best he could. "I'd listen to her if I was you."

"Why the hell do you think I'm out here?" Matt took another swig from his beer. At this rate, Mason would have to make a special delivery.

"Why the hell are you here anyway?"

Cooper held up the pastry box. "Your wife requested a few things. I'm guessing that sweet tooth has really kicked into overdrive."

Matt shook his head then took another sip of his beer as he settled back into his chair. "She doesn't want to eat them; she wants to taste them."

"Not following."

"She can't be at the bakery to control everything so she's bringing the bakery to her."

Realization dawned on Cooper, and he had to give Shay credit for her sneaky creativity. "So basically, I'm an accomplice to her spying on how Louise is doing."

"Exactly. Now let's just hope the lime to sugar ratio in the key lime pie cupcake is right or I might have to handcuff her to the bed."

"Sounds kinky."

"Trust me there is no kink going on in this house."

Cooper snorted. "Won't let you touch her, huh?"

"I'd rather not talk about it."

"That's a yes."

"I tell her she's beautiful, she tells me I'm a liar because 'how could I find a whale attractive?'"

"She's never seen a whale in person. Beautiful creatures."

"I don't care about the fucking whales or if she feels like one. She could be the size of the whole damn state, and I wouldn't care." Matt ran a hand through his hair, the tension obvious in the straining veins of his arms. "She's carrying my child, and while she looks in the mirror and sees the weight gain and the swelling, all I see is the beauty of it."

"Have you told her that?"

"What's the point? She won't listen."

"Then make her."

Matt choked on a laugh. "Have you met my wife? Five-foot-nothing brunette who thrives on not listening to me?"

"That's because you're usually barking orders. I wouldn't listen to you either."

"When have you ever listened to me?"

Cooper spent much of his childhood defying his older brother and refusing to follow his example, preferring to do things his own way, but there were plenty of times when Matt's past advice came in handy. Cooper might not have listened in the moments they were meant for, but the words had stuck with him and became beneficial at other times.

"A lot actually," Cooper admitted.

The tension that Matt had been consumed with began to ease, his shoulders relaxing in the midday sun. His lip tilted in a half-smile. "You're not just saying that to make me feel better?"

Cooper patted Matt on the shoulder. "When you stop barking at people, you actually have some pretty decent advice. So, like you told me when my wallet and phone were stolen in Barcelona and I didn't have access to my bank account for days, don't let one bump ruin the whole journey. All this is"—Cooper motioned to Matt—"is a bump. Probably one of many, but once you get to the top, it's smooth sailing on the way down. Give her space. Let her just be pregnant. She doesn't need you telling her what to do. I'm sure she knows her body better than you anyway."

Matt cocked an insinuating eyebrow.

"Bad choice of words," Cooper said. "This whole advice thing isn't really my forte. That's Mason's department. Just go with it."

"Funny because I was just wondering when the hell you got so smart."

"I think somewhere between Barcelona and Istanbul."

Matt shook his head, but he couldn't cover up the smile tugging generously at the edges of his mouth. "Still a smartass."

"In this family, it's my only defense." He held up the box of pastries. "I better get these to her. You going to be okay?"

"I'll be fine. Will you be here for a while?"

"If you need me to be."

"I just want to go out on the lake for a little. Clear my head."

"Go."

"I'm not going far. If anything happens just yell for me."

"There you go… being crazy again."

"One day," Matt said, his green eyes pinning Cooper in place, "you're going to be in my shoes, and we'll see who's crazy."

"Nice thought, but we both know that's never going to happen. Wife and kids are not my thing."

"We'll see," Matt said with a cocky smile before walking toward the edge of the lake where his canoe lay.

Cooper didn't even bother yelling after him that he was delusional. There was no point. Matt had already had ideas of Cooper's future in his mind. Too bad his vision couldn't be further from the truth.

Cooper had no desire to get married, and the thought of kids made his lip curl in disgust. Not that he didn't like kids, they were cool, but that was only because they weren't his. If they cried, he could hand them right back to their parents and be done with them. If they got to be too much to handle he could leave and go home. He wasn't tied to them in anyway, and that's the life he preferred. Being free of responsibility and having the freedom to come and go as he pleased.

He watched as Matt rowed out across the lake before going into the house to find Shay. She was in the bedroom, propped up on pillows, a stack of books on her nightstand, a tray of food to her left, and a floor fan pointed directly at her.

Cooper knocked lightly on the door. "Special delivery," he said, holding the box in the doorway before stepping into the room.

"Oh, you're here!" she exclaimed excitedly. "Come in, come in." She motioned her hands toward the box then waved them toward her. "Give me."

"You're not going to bite my head off are you?"

"Of course not."

Cooper had been scared to come up here after talking to Matt, but now his suspicions were confirmed. Shay's foul mood had nothing to do with hormones and everything to do with Matt being overbearing.

"You kicked my brother out."

"Don't even get me started." The happy expression on her face dissolved into pure evil.

Cooper gave her the box to try and snuff out the fuse he just lit. Her smile returned as she flipped the lid open and examined the pastries inside. "Not bad," she said with a nod. "Now for the true test." She picked up the key lime pie cupcake and took a bite.

Cooper stood back and waited for a response, deciding it was best to keep the fact that he had already tried one today and it was delicious.

"A little too sweet. Could use a little more lime juice, but not bad," she said as she moved onto the chocolate stout cupcake that she created using a batch of Mason's beer. "Not sweet enough, but it'll do."

Cooper held back a laugh as she took a bite of every single item in the box and had a minor complaint about each one of them. Shay taught Louise everything she knew and all the recipes Louise was following were created by Shay. But Shay was just like Matt in that nobody could do something better than her. Two micro-managers who hated to ask for help and refused to let go of the reins, it was no wonder they were currently bumping heads.

"Do they pass the test?" Cooper finally asked when Shay closed the lid. "Or do I have to fire Louise?"

"What? Of course not. Louise is the only thing keeping me in business right now."

"Then why are you having me sneak pastries out of the bakery for you to taste test? And why are you critiquing them like you're a judge on some baking reality show."

"I just…"

Cooper crossed his arms over his chest and glanced down at Shay.

"I mean…I…Fine. I'm afraid she's going to get better at baking than me, and when I go back people will be disappointed."

"That's impossible. You know that, right?"

She shrugged. "I guess so."

"Sweet Dreams Bakery is what it is because of you. Nobody can replace you. It's your bakery and your recipes. Stop obsessing over the things you can't control and start focusing on this." He motioned to her ever-growing stomach.

"You sound like your brother."

"Not my fault we come from the same DNA."

"So help me," she said, resting her hands on her belly, but despite the disdain in her tone, a smile spread across her face. "If this little man is anything like his daddy I'm in for some trouble."

While she seemed to be in a good mood, Cooper decided to ask her a question that had been on his mind all day.

"You had a customer today. Sarah Kramer."

Shay's gaze turned on him with purpose. "Stay away from her."

"What? Why?"

"She's not your type."

"How do you know?"

"Just trust me on this one."

"Kind of hard to trust you when you won't give me any information. She seems like a nice girl once you chip away at her hard exterior."

"She is."

"Then what is it? Do you not think I'm good enough for her? Because I'd have you know I'm a pretty decent guy."

"I know that. But you also don't stay in one place for too long, and you've already been home for a lot longer than you planned. Don't start something with her if you don't plan on sticking around."

"I just wanted dinner and a chance to show her a good time. I didn't say anything about some long-term commitment."

"Which is exactly why you need to drop it."

"Do people not go on dates anymore? I know I've been out of the country more than I've been in it, but I didn't think that was an outdated concept—"

"Cooper!" Shay's outburst cut him off, and he looked at her with curiosity. She let out a deep breath then met his eyes. "She has a kid."

Shay might as well have sucker-punched him in the gut. "A kid?"

"Tommy, he just turned seven."

"Seven?"

"Told you she wasn't your type," Shay said and though he agreed with her, he couldn't help but be disappointed.

Chapter 2

Sarah was running late to pick up her son. She was never late, and it's not like she had more orders to fill and process than usual, but somehow time managed to get away from her today.

She blamed it on Cooper Hayes. He had completely thrown a monkey wrench into her daily routine by staring at her with those amazingly blue eyes and asking her one too many questions. And what exactly did he mean when he said she looked like she could use a little fun? She had fun. Maybe not jumping out of planes and zip-lining across a rainforest like she'd heard he had done, but fun no less.

Besides, what gave *him* the right to judge *her*? He didn't know her. Had no idea who she was or what she'd done. So maybe her life wasn't full of late nights and vodka shots, but she was a mom, dammit, and that was all the fun she needed.

She turned into the school parking lot and spotted Tommy standing with his teacher and her good friend, Sophie Reynolds. Sophie looked the picture-perfect version of a first-grade teacher in her baby blue shirt tucked neatly into a pair of tan pants and accented with a gold skinny belt and gold flats. The repurposed vintage necklace Sarah had made her for teacher appreciation week popped against the baby blue button down and gave the outfit that extra something.

"I'm so sorry I'm late," Sarah said as she pulled alongside them. She put the car in park and got out, joining them on the sidewalk. "I lost track of time." Sarah went right to Tommy, getting down on her knee and taking his red lunch bag. "Sorry, buddy."

"It's okay, Mom. Miss Sophie kept me company."

Sarah stood up and turned to her friend. "Thank you. I—"

Sophie held her hand up. "It's okay." Her friendly smile spreading across her face. "It happens. Besides, I couldn't have asked for better company," she said to Tommy who blushed instantly. Sophie turned back to Sarah. "Rough day?"

"Strange is more like it." Unlike Sarah, Sophie grew up in Red Maple Falls. She knew everyone and everything about them. She'd definitely know Cooper. Probably even went to school with him. She debated asking about him, but why? He was just a guy at the bakery who happened to ask her out. So why was it that she couldn't get her mind off of him?

Cooper Hayes preceded his reputation as the worldly, good-looking youngest Hayes brother. He was obscenely confident—bordering the line of arrogance and charming—and she wanted to slap herself for thinking he landed more on the charming end of the spectrum.

Cooper Hayes was everything she didn't need in her life: unpredictable, audacious, self-assured... All problems on their own, but when combined together into a sexy hot package, it was downright lethal.

No matter how tempting he was, she needed to stay away from him. Her life wasn't about her wants. It was about Tommy and what Tommy needed. And the last thing Tommy needed was for her to bring someone into his life he would no doubt fall in love with, only for that person to move on with his life. She wouldn't do that to her son.

She made a vow the day she held him in her arms for

the first time, red-faced and chunky cheeks, that she would always put him first. He was her reason for living, the reason she got up every day and pledged to make it better than the last.

Even though there were nights when she was lonely, all she had to do was look at her son and remind herself of what was important.

"Want to talk about it?" Sophie asked.

She wasn't going to ask Sophie about Cooper because she knew everything she needed to know already.

"It's nothing, really."

"Okay, then." Sophie wasn't one to pry, and Sarah appreciated than more than anything. "I actually talked to my sister a little while ago and she said if I saw you to let you know she has some new pieces in."

Sophie's sister, Ellie, owned Forgotten Treasures Antiques where Sarah got most of the jewelry she repurposed and sold on her online store.

"Perfect. I'll stop by there tomorrow afternoon."

"Mom?" Tommy tugged on her blazer. "Mom?" He bounced up and down with that never-ending dose of energy he had.

"What is it, Tommy?"

He held up a flyer, his shaggy brown hair flopping in his eyes no matter how many times she combed it back into place; she tried again brushing it aside with her fingers. His dark brown eyes, just like her own, stared up at her with lively excitement. His big smile spread wide from one side straight to the other. "Can I go? Please?"

She took the flyer from his hand and read the bold letters. **Bob's Big Adventures**. Beneath it, in smaller print, **for beginners to experts**. *Come join me this summer and discover* *all that Red Maple Falls has to offer. Canoe/kayak lessons, rock climbing adventures, trail survival classes, and so much more. Call today to reserve your spot. Supervised weekly summer programs for children and teens also available. Spots are limited.*

She looked to Sophie to see if she knew anything about it, but Sophie only shrugged.

"So can I, Mom? Please. I promise to be good. Joey is going and I really, really want to go."

"Why don't we talk about this tonight?"

"But Mom!"

"No 'but Mom's.' We'll talk about it tonight. Now get in the car."

His shoulders slumped forward as if he had the weight of the world on his shoulders and dragged his feet to the car in performance worthy exaggeration.

Sarah laughed and shook her head as Tommy got into the passenger seat. "He is too much."

"He's a good kid. You're lucky."

"I am, aren't I?" Somehow in the mystery that was life—her unexpected pregnancy at eighteen—turned out to be the best damn thing that ever happened to her. "I should get going. We still on for Wednesday?"

Every Wednesday night while Tommy was at karate class, they met up for dinner at the Happy Apple, a local restaurant that was known not only for their amazing food and outrageous apple décor, but also for the boisterous redhead who owned the place with her big teddy bear of a husband. It was always a guaranteed entertaining time and gave Sarah an hour a week to be a twenty-six-year-old girl out with a friend for the night.

She loved her son to death, couldn't imagine life without him, but she looked forward to her Wednesday nights when she could unwind a little and not have to worry about homework and messes.

"Of course. I wouldn't want to miss out on my weekly apple cheddar turkey burger. I swear I dream about it."

"Sometimes I wonder what Terry actually puts in her food to make it so addicting."

"What we don't know can't hurt us."

"Good point. Better to remain a mystery."

"Mom, how much longer?" Tommy whined from the car.

"Just a minute," she said to Tommy then turned back to Sophie. "Thanks again for staying with him. It won't happen again."

"Sarah, it's my job and even if it wasn't, I don't mind."

"That's because you're the best."

"Someone has to be," she said with a wink. "See you Wednesday," she called over her shoulder as she turned on her gold flats and headed back toward the school.

"Mom?" Tommy said as she slid into the driver seat. "So have you thought about it? Can I go?"

"I thought I said we would discuss it tonight."

"But that's so far away!"

Sarah hated to say no to her son, but she had been looking forward to their summer together. There was so much she wanted to do and show him, but he was getting to that age when he wanted to do things on his own. He was seven but he might as well have been sixteen. He no longer liked when she gave him a hug in front of his friends or walked him to the main doors of the school. She worried it was her fault that he was becoming fiercely independent. But she also knew that was a good thing, even if it did make her sad.

God, what would she do when he *was* sixteen and driving. She didn't want to think about it. Luckily, she still had time. Though, the past seven years had flown by so fast she gave herself whiplash just thinking about it.

At home, she put the last of the dishes away and hung the dishtowel on the oven rail. Tommy ran into the room at record speed, coming to a skidding halt in front of her.

"The sun is gone so that means it's tonight."

She laughed, always amused by the way he viewed things. "Yes, I suppose that's what that means."

"Can I go to the camp? Pretty please, Mom. With whip cream and a cherry on top. Please. Please."

She held up her hand to stop the nine hundred more pleases she knew were coming. "Let me talk to Joey's mom and get a little more information."

His big eyes widened, pure joy spreading across his adorable little face before he broke out into a happy dance.

"I didn't say yes," she reminded him.

"But you didn't say no." His lip quirked in that mischievous way of his before he spun on his heel. "I'm going to call Joey right now."

"Is your homework done?" she called after him.

"I just have to read, but I can do that later."

"No, you can do that before you call Joey."

"But Mom!" For some reason, her son hated to read. He preferred to be outside playing in the mud or building small towns with his Legos. Getting him to sit still for twenty minutes every night to read a few pages of a book was borderline torture. She'd tried everything to make it more enjoyable for him. Even bringing him to the library to pick out his own books. He didn't care about the characters who had adventures within the pages when he could be making his own adventures.

"No buts," she said, her hand landing on her hip and making her wonder when exactly she became her mother.

Tommy let out a loud exaggerated breath. "Fine." He stomped away as if he was being sent to his doom. She turned back to the sink, resting her hands on the cool surface and letting out her own breath, thankful the fight was only short-lived.

Wednesday couldn't get here fast enough.

***

Sarah dropped Tommy off at karate and decided to walk to the Happy Apple which was only around the block down Main Street. It was a gorgeous evening, despite the cold breeze that blew every now and again, reminding all of Red Maple Falls that it wasn't uncommon to be hit with a snowstorm in the middle of spring. She just hoped she'd seen the last of the snow until next season.

It was six o'clock on a Wednesday, and Main Street was already dead. Only a few cars were parked along the road. Sarah passed Sweet Dreams Bakery and couldn't help a glance through the window. Louise, a sweet girl with a bubbly personality, was wiping down the counters, and there was no sign of Cooper Hayes—not that she wanted there to be. At least she didn't think she did.

Even if he was behind the counter it's not like she would've gone in to talk to him. She was acting like a school girl with a crush, and it was ridiculous. She was far from a school girl and the last thing she needed was to involve herself with someone who was known not to stick around.

As she approached the Happy Apple, she spotted Sophie heading in. She called out to her and gave a wave.

"Hey," Sophie said as she got closer. "Where's your

car?"

"Over at the karate studio. Thought I'd walk."

"Burning off the calories before you eat them. Smart."

"That actually wasn't even my intention, but let's pretend it was."

"I won't tell if you won't," Sophie said with a smile as she opened the door of the restaurant. The delicious smells of spices and herbs greeted them as they stepped inside.

"I'll be right there," Terry, the owner, called out from the kitchen. She wiped her hands on a dish rag that hung from her apron as she walked on sky high black heels to meet them. Her red hair was puffed up high on her head—a sight that always made Sarah wonder how many cans of hairspray she went through in a week. Leopard print sleeves poked out from her apple decorated apron, and her huge smile was lined by bright red lipstick. "If it isn't my two favorite girls."

"I bet you say that to everyone," Sarah said, giving Terry a hug.

Terry didn't skip a beat, giving a feisty tilt of her head. "Maybe. But you're all my favorites for different reasons."

"I'll take it," Sophie said as she was engulfed in Terry's embrace.

"You're usual table?" Terry asked as she pulled back, and the girls nodded. They had been coming every Wednesday since the beginning of the school year after they'd met during a parent teacher conference and had hit it off.

Sophie was the kind of teacher for Tommy that Sarah had dreamed of—smart, attentive, willing to go that extra mile, warm, and above all, friendly.

So many people who lived in Red Maple Falls were

born and raised, and Sarah found it hard to make friends. She felt like everybody was already settled with their lives and the people they surrounded themselves with, so when Sophie had asked her if she'd like to get dinner one night, Sarah had jumped on it.

That one night turned into a weekly occurrence, and Sarah was grateful to Sophie for accepting an outsider into her life.

It had been hard for Sarah when she left the comforts of her parent's house and went out on her own with Tommy. Though it was freeing, being away from the only place she'd ever known, it was also scary and lonely. While she wasn't a fan of the people she grew up with and most had dropped her when she became pregnant at eighteen, there was still a level of comfort with the familiar that she didn't always have in Red Maple Falls. Until recently.

They sat down at the table, and Terry went to hand them menus then pulled them back. "I don't know why I even bother." She nodded toward them. "Apple cheddar turkey burger. One with sweet potato fries and the other regular fries."

"You got it," Sarah said. "And also."

"Glass of cabernet for you Soph and a water with lemon for you Sarah, right?"

"Right."

"Anything else?"

"Nope, that'll do," Sarah said. "Thanks, Terry. If you can get away for a minute, join us."

"I might take you up on that offer. My bunions are killing me today."

Sarah and Sophie laughed. There was no beating around the bush with Terry. If she had a thought, it came out with no censorship or sugar coating. At first it had taken Sarah aback, but now she found it refreshing.

Terry gave them a wave; the repurposed bracelet made of vintage brooches and watches she had bought from Sarah clanked against her other bangles.

Sarah loved seeing her pieces out in the world, especially worn by people whose opinions she valued.

"So what's new?" Sophie asked as she laced her fingers together and rested her hands on the table.

Sarah went to answer when her eyes were drawn to the sexy-as-sin man who'd just walked through the door. Surrounded by apple décor, he stood out like the perfect male specimen that he was, that carefree air radiating from him in delicious waves.

"What are you looking at?" Sophie asked, turning in her seat before Sarah could stop her. Sarah could feel the heat filling her cheeks as Sophie turned back to her.

"Cooper Hayes?" Sophie said with a lifted eyebrow. "Care to explain?"

"No," Sarah said just as Cooper's blue eyes spotted her from across the room. She knew she should look away, but their eyes were like two magnets, and no matter how hard she tried to resist the pull she couldn't.

His lip curved up at the corner that was part cocky and part charming—a combination that was downright lethal. She swallowed down the strange desire that suddenly consumed her and found the strength to look away.

"Ladies," he said, his voice smooth as silk as he stepped up to their table.

"Cooper," Sophie said. "It's been a long time."

"It has. Tell me, how do you two know each other?"

"I'm her son's teacher."

Sarah's eyes darted to Cooper. That day at the bakery she managed not to mention her son once. Now it was out there in the open, and she knew with this knowledge he'd never look at her again. Being a mother was a responsibility, and rumor had it, Cooper Hayes ran from responsibilities.

"I'm not interrupting a meeting or anything, am I?" Cooper asked, and Sarah was surprised he didn't look like he was searching for an excuse to bolt.

"Not at all. How have you been?"

"Couldn't be better. Surprised I haven't seen you around. I've been home for nine months now." He spoke to Sophie, but his eyes kept lingering on Sarah. She could feel the heat of his gaze penetrating her skin.

"Decided to give up the gypsy lifestyle?"

"It's only temporary," he said, and for some reason that response hit Sarah low in the gut, spreading disappointment through her. "I was hoping to take Sarah here out to dinner while I'm home, but she told me she doesn't have time for fun. Yet here she is, out, having dinner."

"I have to eat," she said, hoping with all that she had that Terry would pop out of the back and grab Cooper's ear.

Sophie's eyes stayed on her, filled with curiosity and unspoken words that said *don't think we're not talking about this later.*

"I guess it's not about not having time and more about not having time for me," Cooper said.

"Something like that."

Cooper grabbed a chair from the empty table behind him, spun it around so the back was facing forward and straddled it.

"Did we say you could join us?" Sarah asked.

"If I would have asked you would have said no."

"Ding ding, we have a winner."

Cooper turned his attention to Sophie. "Is she always like this?"

Sarah gave her a look across the table.

"Like what?" Sophie asked.

"A little rude. Kind of uptight."

"I beg your pardon?" Sarah exclaimed, wanting to smack the smug look off his pretty face.

"I've actually never seen her like this, so that begs the question... What did *you* do to her?"

Cooper's hands shot up. "Whoa. Don't go gathering the town folk on me now. I didn't do anything other than try to have a conversation with her. Apparently like fun it's not something she's too fond of."

"I am sitting right here," Sarah said.

Terry walked over with their drinks, and Sarah wished she ordered something stronger than lemon water. Sophie's wine was looking damn good, and if she didn't have to drive her son home in an hour, she would have grabbed it before Sophie had a chance.

"Cooper my boy!" Terry said with clear admiration as Cooper stood up and gave Terry a hug, lifting her off the ground and causing her to squeal. Terry swatted his chest as he put her down. "You're so bad."

The jerk actually had the nerve to wink at Sarah. She rolled her eyes, but only to hide the sudden flush of heat that rushed through her body.

Get it together, Sarah. It was a wink. I bet he winks at hundreds of girls every day.

After the disaster that was Tommy's father, she thought she was immune to men, especially ones with too much confidence and a charming smile, but Cooper was cracking her exterior and getting under her skin in a way no man had ever been able to before.

"You here to pick up your parent's order?" Terry asked him.

"I am."

"Let me go grab that for you. Walt was just packing it up." Terry walked away, and Cooper rested his hand on the back of the chair, spinning it around and putting it back where he took it from.

"While it's been a pleasure, ladies, I do have to get going."

"Shame," Sarah said, but had no idea why she did. There was just something about him that made the polite, friendly girl disappear. Maybe it was because he was a temptation, and it was easier to keep him at arms-length, and the only way to do that was to make herself unappealing.

But when he looked at her with those bright baby blue eyes, a smile tugging generously at the edge of his mouth, she had a feeling her plan wasn't working at all. If anything, it was doing the exact opposite.

Cooper turned his amused gaze onto her. "I know how much you're enjoying my company so I'm sorry to cut it short, but the invitation still stands."

She swallowed down the rising desire that was screaming for her to stop doing everything she was supposed to and start doing what she wanted and looked him straight in the eyes. "Don't hold your breath."

He smirked, those luscious lips parting. "For you, baby, I will."

His statement knocked the wind right out of her. Before she could say a single word, he walked away, grabbing his to-go order from Terry and heading out into the night.

She sat there, momentarily paralyzed by his lingering presence, those words, echoing in her mind.

"Talk," Sophie said, her voice penetrating the fog Cooper left her in.

"There's nothing to talk about."

A loud laugh burst from Sophie, and she smacked a hand over her mouth. "Liar."

"I went to the bakery on Monday, like I always do, and he was working behind the counter. He was smug and arrogant and flirtatious."

"And he got to you."

"No."

"Then why are your cheeks so red?"

"It's hot in here."

"Try again."

"Fine. He got to me. I mean, have you seen the guy? It should be illegal to be that attractive."

"I've known him my whole life, so I'm kind of immune to it, I guess."

"Then you know he is the last thing I need in my life."

Sophie took a sip of wine, but Sarah could see the thoughts on her face that she was keeping to herself.

"What?" Sarah asked.

She put her glass down, laced her fingers together and rested her hands on the table like earlier. "Cooper Hayes is a player. He's not known for being with a girl for longer than a week. But. He has a reputation of being a god in bed."

"Good to know," Sarah said, her tone dripping with sarcasm. "And that's exactly why I need to stay away from him."

"See, that's where I disagree."

"What are you talking about?"

"Sarah," Sophie said, reaching across the table and resting her hand on hers. "Everything you do is for Tommy. The only reason we have dinner every Wednesday night is because Tommy is at karate."

"He's my number one priority."

"I know that, and you're a great mother because of that, but don't you think it's time to give yourself a little break? Tommy's a good kid, and you having a social life isn't going to change that. I'm sorry, but I agree with Cooper. You deserve a little fun."

"And what? You think Cooper Hayes is the answer?"

Sophie picked up her wine and took a small sip, her eyebrows raised over the glass as she gave a subtle nod.

"You said yourself he's a player. He doesn't do relationships."

"Which is exactly why he's perfect. You need to dip your toes in the pool before you jump in. Why not do it with a man who is clearly taken by you? Not to mention has abs you could break wood on."

"How do you know what his abs are like?"

"People talk. Let's just say that boy isn't lacking in any area."

Sarah wasn't surprised. He looked like he stepped out of a special edition of small-town GQ. He had everything going for him—charm, good looks, sense of humor, and for whatever reason, she was the current obstacle in his game.

Maybe Sophie was right. Maybe it was time she let herself have a little fun.

"I don't want to make you feel like you have to do anything you don't want to," Sophie said. "But if you want fun, Cooper is your man. Just don't let yourself fall in love with him because there is no good that can come from that."

"I wouldn't."

"Good." Sophie held up her glass. "So what do you say? You going to dip your toes?"

Sarah clinked her glass against Sophie's. "Why the hell not?"

Chapter 3

Cooper sat back in the rocking chair on the small front porch of his tiny home, looking out across his parents' farm. The sun had finally melted the last of the winter snow, and pretty soon the hot days of summer would be upon them, which meant he would have been home for almost an entire year.

It's the longest he'd been back home since he was eighteen, and while he loved cross country skiing and snowmobiling, they had lost their appeal after the first month. At least now he could change it up with mountain biking or kayaking. Maybe even a little rock climbing and scuba diving in the lake, but he knew he'd get bored with that, too. It was all stuff he'd done and seen before. He needed something else, something that would keep his wandering mind occupied.

He closed his eyes, letting the midday sun shine down on his face, and cleared his mind. When he was able to stop and appreciate the simplicity of life, he rather enjoyed himself. But it never lasted long. It was only a few minutes before the gears in his head would start churning and convincing him that he was wasting his time sitting around.

"You alive over there?" His dad's voice floated across the field.

"I might be dying of boredom, but it hasn't claimed me just yet."

Jonathon Hayes laughed. He was in his usual khaki shorts with work boots and white socks poking out the top.

He wore a green t-shirt that had the name of the family farm written across his pecs. For a man in his sixties, he was in damn good shape do to all the heavy lifting that came with farm life. The summer still hadn't arrived, but Jonathon Hayes was already sporting a tan. His dirty blond hair filled more and more with gray.

It was a hard pill to swallow—accepting that you and the ones you loved were aging. Cooper had always lived his life in the now, never thinking about the future, always assuming that when he came home everything would be exactly the same. He was beginning to realize it wasn't.

During his last trip, his oldest brother reconnected with the girl he never got over and got engaged to get married— something Cooper thought would never happen. When he got the news, he knew he had to make it to the wedding.

It was only supposed to be a quick trip, but once he got home, surrounded by the people he loved, celebrating new beginnings, something held him back. And when his brother, Mason, asked if he would help get his brewery up and running, he couldn't say no. He had said no so many times over the years, missed out on so much, and even though the desire to leave was always on the edge of his mind, he ignored it so he could help.

Now, with the brewery up and running, his tiny home built, book written, it was only a matter of time before he left this all behind.

"What's up?" he asked as his dad sat down on the steps that led to his red door.

"I have a proposition for you."

Cooper pushed his aviators up on his head and leaned forward, resting his elbows on his knees. "I'm listening."

"You remember Bob Clemons from Big Bob's

Adventures?"

"Of course. You sent me to summer camp there as a kid. Freaking loved it."

"Good, you do remember then. I was worried with all your travels you wouldn't remember that summer."

"That was the summer that kick-started everything." Cooper remembered going on walks through the woods, identifying different animal tracks, learning how to canoe and kayak without his older brothers trying to tip him over. He explored the local caves and fished in the local lakes. After that summer, he knew being stuck inside wasn't for him. He needed to be out in the world, seeing everything that there was. Big Bob made a massive impact on him and who Cooper was today.

He had always meant to stop over there just to talk to the man who had to be in his sixties now, but Cooper never had the time.

"So what's the proposition?" he asked.

"Bob's sister is sick. He's all she has so he needs to head out to California to help take care of her. With him gone, he's short-staffed. He needs someone to fill in for him. Take over one his groups."

"What the hell. I'll do it."

"Really?"

"If I can help give some kid amazing memories like I have, then it's a no-brainer."

"I'll let Bob know. Give him your cell number so he can call you directly and work out all the details."

"Sounds good."

"I'd join you for a while, but I have to go help your grandmother hang a curtain."

"At least she's not trying to stand on something to do it

herself."

"I think she's finally accepted there are some things she just can't do anymore."

"Now if only Grandpa would hurry up. We could all sleep a little easier."

"You're telling me. I'll see you later." Jonathon Hayes gave a wave as he headed down the dirt path that led to the main house.

Cooper was about to head inside when his cell rang. He slipped it out and didn't recognize the number but answered anyway.

"Hey, this is Cooper."

There was silence on the other end, and he was about to hang up when he heard her voice.

"Hi Cooper, it's Sarah."

He sat up straighter, a smile forming on his face. His boring night just got better.

***

Cooper had no intention of going over to Sarah and Sophie's table the other night. Sarah had a kid, and it had raised a red flag when Shay told him, but the minute his eyes settled on hers, he couldn't resist.

She was infuriating in the way she was immune to his charm. How she could turn him down without as much as blinking an eyelash. But the longer he sat there, their bodies mere inches away from each other, he could see the perfectly crafted wall of hers breaking down with each heavy inhale and the beautiful blush that filled her warm golden cheeks.

At first, he thought maybe he imagined it; a girl like her wouldn't have any cracks in her exterior, but then he got the phone call accepting his dinner invitation.

For the second time, she'd rendered him speechless,

and that was not an easy feat. He offered to pick her up, but she preferred to meet at his place.

He texted her directions and sat on his front porch, waiting for her. She told him seven and at a minute to, she pulled down the back road that led to his place. She parked and got out of the car, her long black hair hanging in long loose waves over a black top that cut into a low V and showed off an amazing set of tits.

All the blood rushed from his head to his groin as she stepped around the door, revealing long bronzed legs. Her top was actually a dress that hugged her body like a custom-made glove.

"This is where you live? It's so tiny."

"I don't need much," he said, walking down the porch steps and greeting her with a kiss on the cheek. At first, he thought it might be too forward, but she actually moved into it, surrounding him in a spicy scent that made him sweat.

"I've seen these on TV, but I've never seen one in real life. I'm always amazed at the unique storage ideas."

"You want to come in and look?"

She went to move then stopped. "This isn't some ploy to try and make a move on me, is it?"

"Even if it was, you just ruined it. But it's not. Promise."

"The jury's still out on if I can trust you, so your promise is kind of a moot point, but I'm curious enough to let it slide."

"As long as you're curious enough," he said with a laugh as he pressed a hand to her lower back and led her to the front door. They walked up the two steps to the small porch.

She pointed to the rocking chair. "Do you sit there a

lot?"

"I do. I like being outside. Having a porch, as small as it may be, was a necessity for me."

"Sounds about right."

He opened the door then turned around until her dark eyes were staring into his. There wasn't much room, forcing them to stand close. He could feel her breath on his face, smell the mint from her toothpaste mixing with her spicy scent. "What is that supposed to mean?" he asked.

She visibly swallowed. "You don't seem like the type who likes to be stuck inside for too long."

He reached up, needing to feel her against his skin. Unable to resist any longer, he tucked her hair behind her ear, his finger grazing the curve of her lobe, causing her to shiver.

"That's because I don't." He stood there, getting lost into the inky black pools she called eyes. The desire to kiss her, feel her lips pressed against his, feel her hands wrap around him in desperation was strong.

"Are you going to let me in?" she asked her voice low and husky, causing his dick to throb.

He cleared his throat, bringing himself back to reality and moving aside. "Of course. After you."

She stepped around him, and he didn't follow right away, taking a second to get his head back on straight. He had been with many women, but the desire that she elicited in him was like nothing he had ever known. Resisting his urges was becoming nearly impossible, and he only hoped that when the time came, she wouldn't push him away.

**

After Cooper gave her a short tour of his tiny home, they hopped in his Jeep, and he drove them to the next town over for dinner. She hadn't suggested it, but was grateful. Living in a small town was great and all, but there was absolutely no privacy. If they would have gone to the Happy Apple or Calhoun's everyone in town would be talking about it by morning, and since it was just something she was doing for fun, she'd prefer they stayed under the radar.

She also wanted to make sure that conversation wouldn't get back to Tommy. He was barely seven, and she didn't want to confuse him or allow expectations to be set.

There was no denying that Tommy wanted a dad, and it killed her that her little boy couldn't have what he most desired. His biological father was nothing more than a sperm donor who denied him, and that betrayal was the beginning of her deep-rooted need to keep Tommy protected from others. The last thing she needed was to give Tommy false hope, and it was the main reason why she didn't date.

But she was lonely, and it had been so long since she put herself first. Cooper wasn't the type of person who did relationships. Tonight, she could have a good time, no strings attached, and come morning they could go their separate ways. It was exactly why she finally broke down and called him.

They pulled up to the restaurant thirty minutes later, and Sarah was happy to get out of the Jeep. Being inside, in such close proximity, smelling his delicious scent—a combination of citrus and woods that was profoundly sensual—had her body reacting in ways she couldn't control. Her nipples tightened beneath the silky thin material of her dress, pressing hard against the barely-there lace bra she bought on a whim and never wore until tonight. Her sex throbbed with all the naughty thoughts that popped in and out of her head whenever Cooper's fingers flexed on the steering wheel.

He provoked so many desires inside her, desires she never felt before, just by being in the same vehicle together. She needed to get out, get some air, and cool down.

The refreshing air of late spring was like a welcoming splash of water on her face as she opened the door. Before she could manage to slip out, Cooper jogged over and extended a helping hand.

She accepted, sliding her hand into his, not expecting the spark of electricity that shot through her veins on contact. He smiled that sexy smile, making her wonder if he felt it, too, or if she was just losing her mind.

"You can't fake the chemistry we have," he said.

Nope. Wasn't losing her mind. Whatever was happening between them was strong and intense. He was right, chemistry like that couldn't be faked. She had been in proximity to men plenty of times over the year, occasionally on Monday's at the bakery, every weekday at the school, Thursday's at the bank, and a thousand times at the post office, but not a single one made her as aware of herself and her body as Cooper did.

She couldn't explain the reaction to him—the instant attraction that filled her senses and made her want things she hadn't wanted since she was a naïve teenager. Her plan was simple, but now she was afraid that spending time with Cooper—letting loose and allowing herself a night of no inhibitions—wouldn't be enough. Whatever spell he had on her would only strengthen.

"You okay?" Cooper asked as his fingers laced with hers, and he walked them toward the restaurant.

She nodded and let the fear of the unknown dissipate. Tonight was about having a good time, and after seven years of being celibate, she deserved this.

"I'm good," she said.

"Then shall we?" He opened the door and stepped back to let her walk inside, his hand falling away from hers. The loss of his touch was immediate, making her aware how much she liked holding on to him.

She went in, Cooper right behind her. The hostess greeted them with a beautiful smile. She was young, maybe just entering her twenties, with long blonde hair that fell over her shoulders.

"Two for dinner," Cooper said that charming smirk of his shining bright as if he couldn't help himself.

The girl blushed. "Of course." She grabbed two menus and waved her hand. "Follow me."

When she tried to sit them at a table by the door Cooper pointed to a different table in the far corner hidden away like its own private area.

The girl picked up the menus she'd already placed on the table and walked them over to the secluded spot.

"Your server will be Max; he'll be over shortly."

"Thank you," Cooper said with that sexy lift of his lip that caused the girl's cheeks to flare before she hurried away.

"Do you flirt with all girls or just blondes with nice smiles?" Sarah asked as they took their seats.

"I wasn't flirting," he said.

Sarah laughed, unable to control the outburst. "You don't even realize you do it, do you?"

He leaned forward, capturing her attention with eyes as rare and as beautiful as blue spinel. "Being nice and flirting are two totally different things. Besides, the only girl I want to flirt with tonight is sitting right in front of me."

If she thought she was immune to his charm, she was

sadly mistaken as heat flared across her chest.

"Which begs the question... Why'd you call?"

"What do you mean?" She asked, fidgeting with her hands and placing them in her lap to keep him from seeing.

"You were so resistant to the idea of having dinner with me the last time we spoke, then next thing I know you tracked my phone number down and were begging me to go out with you."

"Begging?" She choked on a laugh. "Oh, there was no begging."

He crossed his arms across his chest, making his biceps bulge against his navy-blue Henley that only made his eyes that much bluer. "I think there was."

"Maybe in your dreams."

His lip quirked at the corner. "You're probably right."

An excited chill shook her body at the thought of him dreaming about her. Someone brought over water and disappeared. Sarah picked up the glass and took a sip while she gathered her courage.

"So you've been dreaming about me?" she asked, trying not to let it be obvious that the thought made her sex throb and her nipples tighten.

He nodded, picking up his own water. When he put the glass down his lips gleamed against the dim light, and she wondered what it would be like to taste them.

"And what was I doing in your dreams?"

He laughed, and the noise was pure amusement with sexual undertones. "Let's just say you blew my mind."

Heat exploded inside of her, a raging inferno of desire that burned so intense and bright she didn't know if she'd ever be able to get it under control. "Oh," she managed before taking another healthy sip of her water and wishing the waiter would hurry up so she could get a glass of wine.

Cooper reached across the table, taking her hand and turning it over. He ran a finger across her palm, causing a million sparks to ignite only adding to the already uncontrollable fire.

"Now that that is clear, tell me, Sarah, why'd you finally cave?"

She could be honest with him, get rid of all the pretenses, but what would he think of her if she admitted to wanting a night of unadulterated fun?

"I thought it was time to let lose a little, and you seem like you know a thing or two about that."

A knowing look crossed his masculine features. "You have no idea," he said just as the waiter approached them. Cooper let go of her hand and leaned back in his chair.

They ordered their drinks—a pinot grigio for her and one of his brother's beers the restaurant had on tap for him—and the waiter promised to get right on that before disappearing again.

"So, what's your son like?" Cooper asked.

She swallowed down the uncomfortable lump that formed in her throat. "Let's keep our personal lives out of this, okay?"

"Then how am I going to get to know you?"

"We both know the only reason you asked me out was not to get to know each other."

His baby blue eyes caught hers and softened. "That's where you're wrong. There is no question that I want to get to know you intimately, but I also want to get to know who you are as a person. What can I say? I'm intrigued by you, Sarah."

"Then I have one rule."

"I'm all ears."

"My son is off limits. It's just—"

"I get it. Momma Bear protecting her cub."

"Exactly."

"I can respect that.

"Thank you."

The waiter brought over their drinks, and Sarah pushed her water glass away, thankful for the liquid courage in front of her. Though, the longer she sat there, talking with Cooper, the less and less she felt like she needed it. He was easy to talk to. He didn't seem surprised by anything she said, even if on the inside she was shocked at hell at the honesty coming out of her mouth.

"Now," she said, "do *you* have any topics that are off limits?"

He put his glass down and leaned back in the chair. "I'm an open book ready to be read."

She laughed.

"What's so funny?"

"It's just that I've heard the Hayes men are super smooth, and that was…well…weak."

"Is that so?"

"Oh yeah. I mean it could've been worse. You could've said something like you were ready to be devoured in one sitting."

"I kind of like the sound of that."

She pointed at his glass. "Drink your beer."

"Wow, you really are a Mom."

"Sorry. Sometimes it just comes out."

"Don't apologize. It's pretty adorable."

She bit her cheek to try to control the smile that was forcing its way across her face. "There is nothing adorable about motherhood. There are times when an entire day will pass before I realize I had maple syrup on my shirt from breakfast."

Cooper shrugged. "You were just saving it for later."

She choked on her wine and covered her mouth with her hand. "You're funny."

"That's what I've been told." He pushed his glass out of the way and leaned forward. "I know you're a mom, but tell me something else about you. Like what do you do for a living?"

That was a topic she could jump on. Plus, it was a great way to get away from the Mom subject that she promised herself she wouldn't discuss. "I repurpose vintage jewelry into one-of-a-kind pieces and sell them in my online store."

"Now that's not something you hear about every day. How'd you get started?"

"My grandfather liked to bring things 'back to life' as he would say. He mainly restored old bikes, radios, clocks, signs… pretty much anything that didn't involve a motor. I used to sit in his shop and watch him. He'd let me play with the pieces he didn't need, and that's when I made my first bracelet. From there I'd use pretty much anything to make jewelry."

"He sounds like an awesome guy."

"Yeah… he was." Tears pressed at the back of her eyes, just like they always did whenever she thought about her grandpa. He was the one man—other than her father—she could count on for anything, no questions asked. When he died, it was like a part of her died, too.

A gentle hand rested on hers, and she looked up, catching Cooper's eyes just as he squeezed.

"How long has it been?" he asked.

"Seven and a half years. He passed away when I was six months pregnant." The tears pooled in her lids, but she held them back as best she could. "He was so close to meeting his great grandson, but he couldn't hold on any longer."

"How'd he...?"

"Complications from diabetes."

"I'm sorry. I'm sure he would be really proud of you."

She took her hand back and swiped at the tears, angry with herself for letting them fall. "Look at me," she said with a laugh. "We're supposed to be having fun, and I'm a blubbering mess. Tell me something about you. I know you travel a lot. How do you make a living?"

"I'm a travel blogger."

She picked up her napkin and dabbed her eyes. "You get paid to blog about travelling?"

"I do. I also get paid by advertisers since my social media sites have large followings."

"Do you have any idea how many people would kill for that sort of opportunity?"

"Trust me, I know, and there isn't a single day that I take it for granted. But it's not all it's chocked up to be. I've stayed in some pretty grimy places, gotten food poisoning a few times, and even got mugged."

"That's awful."

"I consider myself pretty lucky, since it only happened once. When you're in foreign countries, unfamiliar with the language, travelling alone, you might as well put a target on your back. Most people are kind and helpful, but just like anywhere, you have your bad seeds."

"How many countries have you been to?"

"Seventy-four."

Sarah inhaled her wine instead of swallowing, causing

her to cough. "Seventy-four?"

"Yup."

"That's insane. Counting the U.S, I've only been to four."

"What are the other three?"

"The Philippines every summer until I was sixteen to visit my Mom's family."

"The Philippines is beautiful."

"You've been?"

"For three amazing weeks a few years ago. I visited The Banaue Rice Terraces, went to Luzon to see Mount Mayon, and my personal favorite, The Puerto Princesa Underground River."

An uncontrollable smile formed as Sarah met Cooper's gaze. "That's one of my favorite places. My uncle brought me there when I was thirteen, and I had never experienced something so fun and amazing. The place itself was beautiful, but what I remember most is how I felt when I was there. After that I swore to myself that when I got older I would travel more so I could discover new places and recapture that feeling."

"Did you?"

She shook her head. "My son is my life. Traveling was no longer an option. Not when I was working, trying to put myself through school, and take care of Tommy."

"I bet being a mom captured that feeling a few times. Or at least something close."

She smiled, realizing how right he actually was. "Yes, I guess it has."

"What were the other two countries?"

Sarah was grateful for Cooper's ease at steering the conversation back on track. "Canada and Germany. Canada on a family road trip when I was eleven and Germany when I was seventeen to visit my brother."

"Is he in the military?"

"No, software engineer. He works for a North American company, but they have offices over there, and he always wanted to live abroad, so when the opportunity arose, he jumped on it. He's been there ever since. Ten years now."

"He's older than you, obviously."

"By six years."

"Do you ever miss him?"

"He comes home for Christmas if he can and a few days in the summer if we're lucky. Because of our age difference we never really had a super close relationship. When he hit his teens, he was never really home." She tucked her hair behind her ear then looked up at him. "What about you and your siblings? You all seem really close."

"We are. Matt, is almost ten years older than me, but he's always been there. I appreciate it now, not so much when I was younger. It was like having another dad to answer to."

"Are you the baby in the family?"

"Nope. That would be Daisy who lives in New York. She's an actress... or trying to be. She's had small roles off Broadway, but she's still waiting on her big break."

"What aren't you saying?" Sarah asked.

"What do you mean?"

"There's a tone in your voice when you talk about her that I can't quite decipher, but it tells me you have more to say on the matter."

He raised an eyebrow, and when it settled back into place he let out a breath. "It's just... she had a good thing going here until she up and left after graduation without telling anyone."

"I would think you of all people would understand."

He ran a hand through his hair. "I do… and I don't. I get following a dream, but hurting people in the process isn't how you go about it, so I guess in that aspect, even though it's been four years, I'm still a little disappointed in her for that."

"Have you ever told her?"

He laughed and shook his head. "It wouldn't matter. Daisy does what she wants no matter what anyone says, and I have a feeling that's why she just took off. She didn't want anyone to stop her. I just hope in the end it will all be worth it."

"What about you? Has it all been worth it? The travelling I mean."

"I feel a little guilty for missing holidays and birthdays. Daisy's graduation…"

Sarah watched as Cooper's eyes dropped to the table. While he wasn't frowning she could see a subtle shift in the set of his mouth. "I see," she said.

"See what?"

"You think if you came to her graduation you would have been able to stop her."

"How do you do that?" he asked, staring at her like she just figured out the secret to life.

"So, I'm right."

"How do you know something I've never said out loud?"

"Some would say it's a mom thing, but I've always been good with reading people."

His baby blue eyes locked on hers, darkening to a seductive shade of navy. "What am I thinking right now?" he asked his voice husky and suggestive.

Her teeth slid over her bottom lip as heated desire coursed through her body. "I'd rather not say."

"Come on, Sarah. Tell me."

With the wine giving her the courage she would normally lack, she met his suggestive gaze with her own. "That you'd rather skip out on dinner and bring me back to your place."

He pulled at the collar of his shirt, and she smiled, knowing that her self-assured honesty was affecting him.

"Is that what you want?"

She eased back in her chair, trying to seem cool, despite the raging fire in her veins. "I mean we did drive all this way, and I'm kind of hungry."

His jaw ticked, giving her a power she never knew she possessed or ever craved.

"I promise it'll be worth the wait," she said with a seductive swipe of her tongue across her top lip. She had no idea who this vixen was who took control of her, but she was kind of loving her.

Cooper tilted his head from one side to the other like he was releasing tension. "If that's what you want," he said his voice gruff and sexy as hell.

She wanted to rip his shirt off and see those abs for herself. She wanted to taste his lips and see if he tasted as sinful as he looked. Most of all, she wanted to feel his hands on her, sliding across her bare skin and exploring her body like he explored countries.

But she also didn't want their conversation to end, because despite the sexual attraction that was radiating off of them at unprecedented speed, Cooper Hayes was interesting, and she had never been more intrigued.

Chapter 4

Cooper shifted in the chair, trying to adjust the rock-solid erection that was pressing harshly against the fly of his jeans. He'd never been so easily aroused, but seeing the seduction in Sarah's eyes, the desperate desire that she tried to hide beneath that dark sultry gaze, he'd lost control. He couldn't stop thinking about those perfect tits that peeked out just enough over the neckline of her black dress. He tried to imagine her nipples, debating if they would be an erotic dark pink or a beautiful shade of brown.

He hoped by the end of the night he would put an end to the mystery. Also help cure him of his current dry spell.

For a minute there, he thought his dick was broken. He'd gone on dates when he'd first come home, but the meaningless conversation used as a segue to meaningless sex started to bore him —a concept he couldn't even begin to fathom, no less understand.

Now, he knew nothing about him was broken. He'd never been more primed and ready to go in his life. Maybe he was just looking for something different, for someone who he actually enjoyed spending time with and didn't view their conversation as a stepping stone to sex.

As much as he wanted to bring Sarah back to his place, he was just as happy to sit here, eating dinner and talking with her. She was fascinating. The fact that she didn't let anything stop her from going to college, not even a baby, and that she managed to create a business from the ground up was a testament to the kind of person she was. Driven, brave, and undeterred.

"I got lucky," she said in reference to her business, but Cooper knew that was her being modest.

"How so?"

"Bex Shepard was photographed wearing one of my pieces on a red carpet, and after that my demand sky rocketed."

"The actress?"

She nodded as she forked a piece of chicken into her mouth.

"Now you can't deny how great your work is if one of the biggest up and coming celebrities was caught wearing one of your pieces."

"I didn't realize you were up to date on pop culture."

"I've had a lot of free time on my hands the past few months. TMZ and E News have kept me company a time or two."

Sarah laughed, and it was a sound that he could get used to. It was light and stripped of all the superiority that had consumed her on their first encounter. He decided that he would do everything in his power to make her laugh as often as possible.

"Why do I have a feeling you have no problem finding company?" She took a sip off of her second glass of wine.

"I guess I've gotten picky."

"Oh," she said, her eyes darting down to her plate. The moment of shyness was short lived when she cleared her throat and looked back up at him. "Tell me more about your travels."

"What do you want to know?"

"Anything. Everything." She slid her teeth over her plump bottom lip, nibbling on it for a moment before releasing it. "What were you doing this time last year?"

"Chasing the cheese," he said with a smile.

"Chasing the what?"

"In England, in Gloucestershire at Coopers Hill, they have an annual event where people chase a nine pound round of Double Gloucester **cheese** down the hill."

"For what purpose?"

"To catch it."

"What do you get if you catch it?"

"The cheese," he said with a laugh. "Other people have walked away with sprained ankles, a couple cuts, and bruises. I got some guy's elbow to the eye and walked away with a nice shiner, but it was totally worth it."

"All that for cheese that's been rolled down a hill and probably touched by a hundred dirty fingers?"

"If you catch it, you also get bragging rights. It's not about winning; not much in life is about that. It's about the experience and being able to say that you were a part of something. To me that means so much more than winning."

"That's a good way to look at life. Nowadays people are so focused on being the best at everything."

"I grew up with five siblings with parents and grandparents who allowed us to make mistakes. Never put too much pressure on us to be the best at anything. All they cared about was that we were grateful, courteous, and kind to others. Besides, my brother Matt wins everything. I gave up on winning a long time ago and let him enjoy the glory. I don't need wins to be happy."

"What do you need? To be happy that is?"

He held up his glass. "A good beer, good food, and a good conversation. Honestly, I couldn't ask for more."

The waiter came over and cleared their plates. "Would

you like anything else this evening? Dessert maybe?"

"We'll look at a menu, sure."

"Oh no," Sarah said, waving her hand.

"I know it's not Monday," he said, and she met his eyes across the table. "But come on, Sarah. Live a little."

"I guess we can look."

The waiter nodded and walked away with their finished plates before coming back and handing them the short menu.

Cooper didn't even look at it. "See anything you like?" he asked, sliding it across the table.

Her eyes scanned over the slip of paper encased in a black leather holder. Her tongue dabbed at her lip and her eyes sparkled with desire. Something definitely caught her eye.

"So what will it be?" he asked.

"I couldn't."

"Oh, but you could, and you will."

"I guess I can add some extra time to the treadmill tomorrow."

Cooper smirked. "What I have planned for later, you won't need to."

She sucked in a jagged breath that had him debating if they should get the dessert to go.

"Have we made a decision?" The waiter asked, looking to Cooper who nodded to Sarah.

Cooper leaned forward. "Come on Sarah you know you want it." He was aware of the sexual undertones in his words and by the flush on her chest, she was too.

"Chocolate lava cake with vanilla ice cream, please," she said in a rush then slumped back in her chair as if the decision took a lot out of her.

"Good choice," the waiter said as he scooped up the menu and headed off to the kitchen.

"You're a bad influence," she said; she had no idea how happy that statement made him.

"Sometimes bad is good."

"Or it's just bad."

He laughed. "Okay, Debbie Downer, let's take it down a notch."

She tucked a long strand of black hair behind her ear. "Sorry. Sometimes I can't help it."

"You don't have to apologize. Just promise me one thing."

"What's that?"

"When given the choice to order dessert, order the damn dessert."

Her lips quirked. "If I followed that mantra I wouldn't fit into my pants."

"I think it's a small price to pay for a few moments of joy."

"Says the man who can probably eat anything he wants without gaining an ounce."

He rubbed his stomach. "What can I say? Good genes."

"Asshole," she joked.

The waiter returned with the dessert and placed it on the table with two spoons before leaving them again. Cooper waited for Sarah to dig in first, sitting back and watching her. She hesitated for only a moment before picking up the spoon and taking a generous portion.

As she brought it to her mouth, her eyes slipped shut and as she closed her lips around the spoon, her body relaxed and the most content smiled played at the edges of her mouth.

"Oh my god, that should be illegal. You have to try it."

"I'm rather enjoying watching you eat it."

She rolled her eyes before picking up the other spoon and holding it out to him. "Eat."

"Yes, ma'am," he said with a laugh as he took the spoon from her, wondering if she'd be just as bossy in the bedroom.

***

Sarah sent a text to Gina, Joey's Mom, to check on Tommy. He'd stayed over at Joey's house before, but Sarah was always home, never far away just in case. Tonight was the first night she allowed herself to go out while Tommy was in the care of someone else, and while she was able to push the guilt from her mind at dinner now that she was in the Jeep, waiting for Cooper to get in the driver's side, she had a moment of guilt.

Her phone buzzed with a new message as Cooper got in the car and engulfed her in that scent that made her hungry for him.

Gina: He's just fine. The boys are watching The Lego Movie and eating popcorn.

Sarah: Thanks, Gina.

Gina: No worries.

"Everything okay?" Cooper asked as he turned the key in the ignition.

She tucked her phone back into her bag, letting the guilt float away. Tommy was at his best friend's house, watching his favorite movie and eating one of his favorite snacks. She had nothing to worry about. Gina was as attentive a mother as she was, and she trusted her to make sure Tommy was safe and content.

There was no reason why she couldn't have tonight.

"Everything is great."

He put the truck in drive and turned out of the parking lot. He found her hand on her lap and laced his fingers with hers. Feeling bold after the two glasses of wine, she inched their intertwined hands to her bare thigh.

She caught his glance out of the side of her eye and turned to meet it. There was shock in those baby blues, but also raw, hot desire. She swallowed at the intensity and then unlinked her fingers, letting his hand lay flat on her leg, warm, strong, and arousing.

He let it stay there for a while as if he was waiting for her to change her mind. But she stood by her choices, and she stood by this, wanting desperately for him to touch her.

Slowly, he began to massage her heated flesh, sending a ripple of need to her core. Every caress broke down a door she had long shut until all the inhibitions that had plagued her were gone.

His fingers inched beneath the hem of her dress, working their way up and causing her to suck in a ragged breath. Goosebumps erupted on her skin, a sensual chill running down her spine. Her nipples tingled and hardened in desperation. Her focused and resolute mind fogged up with an insatiable craving.

Moisture pooled between her legs as he continued to inch ever closer to her forbidden flesh. He didn't look away from the road as his thumb brushed the lace of her panties. She closed her eyes, absorbing the sensations that single touch ignited.

It had been so long since she'd been touched and even then it was nothing worth noting. She wanted to know what it felt like to orgasm, to know that heady need that made people unable to keep their clothes on when they were together.

The more Cooper's thumb rubbed against her the more she realized that tonight she would find out what all the fuss was about. She would finally know why people loved sex so much.

His finger looped into her panties and pulled them aside, exposing her to the open air. His finger slid against her, and her head fell back as a moan slipped from her lips.

"God your wet," he said in awe.

She expected to be embarrassed at his declaration, but instead was more turned on than before. She moved against his finger, showing him what she desired most. He didn't disappoint, dragging his digit through her juices before plunging it inside.

She cried out, her body arching off the seat, pushing her mound against his hand. He pulled out slowly, her walls tightening around him and trying to drag him back in.

"I could make you come," he said, pulling her panties back into place before putting his hand back on the steering wheel as if he didn't just have her seeing stars. "But I'd rather wait until I can see your face."

She sucked in a much needed breath, trying to calm the sensory overload that was racking her body. She adjusted her dress, smoothing it back into place and sitting up in the seat. Her eyes drifted to the bulge in Cooper's pants, happy that she wasn't the only one feeling the aftershocks.

The sexual tension hung in the air, heavy and obvious. They still had a good ten minutes before they were back in Red Maple Falls and another ten before they pulled into Cooper's driveway.

Sarah tried to focus on the road ahead of her and not the clawing desire to reach across the console and release his straining erection. God. Who was she? Sex was always the farthest thing from her mind, but now it was all she could think about.

Every flex of his hand made her think of them roaming her body. Every breath made her hyper aware of him and that finger that was just inside her. She wanted him more than she'd ever wanted anyone before. When they passed the sign welcoming them back to Red Maple Falls she let out a relieved sigh. *So close,* she thought. *So close.*

It was as if her body knew. She shifted in her seat, the slight rub of her panties rubbing against her swollen clit sending an unexpected shudder through her.

"You still wet?" Cooper asked as he turned onto Main Street.

His erotic words, flowing so easily from his mouth, made her even more hot and bothered. She nodded, afraid if she spoke it would come out in a raspy gasp of undecipherable sounds. He rested his hand on her thigh, inching back up to that forbidden spot until his finger ran across lace.

She bowed toward his touch, hungry for more.

Like before, he hooked his finger into the lacy material and pulled it aside. His thumb brushed against her swollen nub, and she cried out at the intense pleasure that consumed her. He rubbed tight toe-curling circles, each one more intense than the last.

She felt the truck speed up, but her mind was too occupied with Cooper's touch to care. She was teetering on the edge when the Jeep came to an abrupt stop. She opened her eyes and was amazed to see that they were in Cooper's driveway already.

He tossed the truck in park and grabbed her face,

drawing her lips to his. He devoured her in a single kiss that far surpassed any kiss she'd ever had. His tongue pushed past the divide, plunging and searching with delicious strokes.

His fingers thrust into her hair, angling her head and deepening the kiss.

Her hands slipped beneath his shirt, discovering his hard, defined abs. She trailed her fingers along his heated skin and rested on his back, urging him closer.

Pleasure rocked into her as his finger pushed inside her. A cry tore from her mouth, but was muffled by Cooper's lips. He pulled back, resting his head against hers. "We should move this indoors," he said between heavy breaths.

She tilted her chin to the side, capturing his lips and moving toward him. He leaned back, and she moved with him. When his back pressed against the driver door, she kicked her leg over his legs, straddling him.

His hands settled on her hips as his tongue slid against hers in an erotic dance of give and take. She vaguely heard the click of the door, the slight cool night air brushing against her skin. He grabbed her ass and slid out of the truck, holding her tight against him, never once breaking his lips from hers.

She wrapped her legs around him tightly as he carried her up the steps and into his tiny home. The door slammed shut behind them, and he pressed her against it.

Never in her life had she done anything like this. It was deliciously wrong, and she didn't want to stop. Not now. Not ever. It felt too good.

His hands roamed up and down her body. She writhed against him, using the heel of her foot to push him closer. A desperate need to feel every inch of him took control.

Her hands ran through his hair, loving the soft feel of the light brown stands before he grabbed her wrists and pinned them above her head, leaving her restricted and vulnerable.

Their mouths crashed together, teeth clashing as their tongues tangled. It was hot and frantic. Sexy and desperate. Beyond any passion Sarah had ever experienced.

Cooper ripped down her dress, dipping his head and dragging his tongue along the black lace of her bra. Her head fell back against the door as he peeled one cup away, releasing her.

"Light brown perfection," he said and before she could ask anything he took the tight bead into his mouth, swirling his tongue around the sensitive flesh. He gently scraped his teeth against the hardened peak, tugging softly.

"Yes, just like that. Please, don't stop," Sarah moaned. White hot bursts of light sparked behind her eyelids as she pressed into him.

"You like that, huh?" Cooper growled as his lips trailed a fiery path over her breasts to the crook between her neck and shoulder, biting and licking before continuing his path.

His lips met hers, his hands cradling her ass as he spun them away from the door and walked her toward his built-in couch. "God, you're making me crazy." He eased her down until her back hit the soft gray cushion, black pillows resting against her arms.

Sarah had never been so turned on in her life. Flaming heat licked its way across every inch of her body, a need so intense it had her core trembling and aching for release.

Cooper came down on top of her, holding his weight above her.

"You have too many clothes on," Sarah said, reaching

for his shirt, greedily tugging at the material and trying to force it out of her way. He reached behind him, grabbing the material, dragging it over his head, and tossing it to the floor.

"Better?" he asked with a sexy quirk of his lips.

"Much."

Her hands went right to his chest, splaying out across the hard muscles. She traced each defined line, staring in amazement and the perfection beneath her hands.

He let her explore for a few moments then grabbed her wrists and pushed them above her head again. "My turn," he said, tugging at her dress.

With a soft moan, he inched her dress down farther until it was nothing but a pile on the floor. An awed smirk spread across his face as he looked down at her in nothing more than a black lace bra and matching panties.

His intense stare, filled with hunger and desire, flicked up and down her body in long torturous glances. She squirmed under the heated craving of his gaze.

She knew she was in great shape, thanks to her dedicated treadmill regime. But being the attention of someone's desire, knowing that he was absorbing every inch of her body, looking as if he were burning it to memory made her unsure of herself.

Her arms instinctively wrapped around her midsection, but Cooper quickly pushed them out of the way. "Don't," he said, so much yearning in that one fervent word. His eyes met hers, pools of navy blue darkened with passion. "The first thing about having fun is to not think. Let go of any insecurities you have because trust me"—his gaze dragged over her body, a red-hot hunger burning bright in his irises—"you have no reason to have any."

Normally, she was able to keep her insecurities bottled

up on the inside, but Cooper had stripped her bare, mind and body. She couldn't hide from him. Not anymore.

The tension that crept into her veins when his hungry eyes turned on her began to loosen. She wrapped her arms around his neck and pushed her fingers through his hair.

Looking up at him, she fell into those beautiful eyes and she was afraid that if they kept talking she would fall further with no return. Cooper Hayes was the type of guy she could fall in love with if she let herself. But she couldn't. Cooper didn't do relationships.

Cooper Hayes was meant to be a good time, and she had to remember that.

She lifted up, brushing her lips against his ever so softly before pulling away. "No more talking," she said then crashed her lips to his in frantic desire, showing him what she really wanted.

He didn't disappoint, of course, taking the lead and scooping her up until she was straddling his lap. His erection pressed insistently against her. The only thing between them was the thin lace of her panties and his jeans that she desperately wanted to rip off.

His hands ran down her arms then found their way to her waist, wrapping around her midsection. She grinded against him, showing him what she desired most as she reached down for his zipper.

He groaned as his head fell back. She was about to get the stubborn button through the hole when he stood up, securing a hand beneath her ass.

A small yelp escaped her lips as he walked her to the ladder that led up to his tiny bedroom. "I need more room than the couch," he said as he released his grip and let her slide down the front of his body. He nodded to the ladder.

"Go."

Knowing what was awaiting her once she got to the top, she didn't waste a second as she placed one foot on the bottom rung and hoisted herself up. By the time she got to the second his hand came around her, halting her advances.

His tongue swirled over the curve of her ass as he pulled the material out of the way. She sucked in a ragged breath as hot need coursed through her body.

"I love these, but they're in the way," he said as his fingers hooked into her panties and ripped them down to her ankles.

There she was, standing on a ladder, completely exposed to this impossible man with an insatiable appetite. She kicked the strips of lace out of the way and went to continue up the stairs when his hands pressed into her stomach, pushing her back to his insistent mouth.

His finger slid through her slick folds, and her hands tightened on the ladder preparing for more of his assault. A loud moan tore from her mouth as his tongue replaced his finger, and a parade of tiny explosions detonated throughout her entire body.

Letting her inhibitions disappear she leaned into that devilish tongue, absorbing every delicious sensation it created. His hands dug into her sides, and she could feel his satisfied moans against her swollen folds.

Her body jerked as his thumb came down on her sensitive button, rubbing slow insistent circles. She felt herself moving toward the edge, a tight coil growing ever tighter with each stroke of his tongue and swipe of his finger.

Gradually a tremor moved up her body pushing her toward the fall. She closed her eyes ready to succumb when a large hand came down gently but with enough force to knock her away from the edge.

Cooper stepped up on the ladder behind her, pressing his body against hers, his mouth brushing her ear. "I told you I want to see your face when you come."

His words sent her spiraling. The need to feel him inside her grew with each breath. She reached behind her, cupping his straining erection. "You need to free him first," she said, forcing herself to keep her voice steady.

In one quick motion, Cooper jumped from the ladder and within seconds was back behind her, bare and eager. His length pressed against her back, and she reached behind her taking him in her hand. She stroked up and down, causing him to groan and making her feel for the first time together in control.

She was used to being in control. It was who she was, but somehow Cooper managed to strip her of it completely, and for once she was okay with letting someone else take the reins.

"After you," he said, his hand resting on her ass and giving it a little push up.

She let him go and climbed the rest of the way until she was at the top, looking down at him and his tiny home beneath him. She crawled to the bed, knowing the space wouldn't accommodate her height.

Cooper stood, his size becoming apparent in the small space. He was bent at a ninety-degree angle as he stalked over to her. His eyes focused and determined. A carefree smile pulled at his lips just as he tackled her to the bed.

"Cooper!" she exclaimed, but couldn't help the laugh that burst from her at the unexpected playfulness.

They wrestled a little, laughing like two teenagers before

he flipped her beneath him and pinned her hands above her head.

She smiled up at him, trying so hard to remember the last time she felt this free. "Why do I feel like you watched a lot of WrestleMania when you were a kid?"

"Because I did."

"Knew it," she said with a laugh.

"I bet you played with Barbie's and had all of their outfits color coordinated."

She tried to hide her smile as she looked away. "Maybe."

He turned her face back to his, tucking her hair behind her ear. She could feel the shift from hot passion to sweet affection. Fear began to overshadow her carefree state. She wasn't ready for the night to end, but it also couldn't become something it wasn't.

She reached down, stroking his incessant erection until the sweet affection turned to pure hot desire. His lips came down on hers hard and demanding. The fear dissipated with each stroke of his tongue.

He dipped his head, taking her nipple into his mouth as he pinched the other between his fingers. Her body arched into his, greedy with want. It took him only seconds to get her wound up again.

She heard the sound of a drawer opening then the rip of a wrapper

She opened her lust heavy eyes as he rolled the condom on then came over her. "No turning back," he said as he glanced down at her.

"Good."

He positioned himself at her slick entrance then caught her gaze just as he thrust inside her. She moaned as she adjusted to his size.

"Shit, baby," he said as his body stilled as if he needed a moment to adjust, too. The veins in his arms bulged, his breaths evening out before he started to move.

Each slow thrust basked her in ecstasy, showing her all that she had been missing out on over the years.

His hand cupped her cheek, his thumb running across her heated skin. "Look at me," he demanded.

She opened her eyes, meeting his blue ones seeing that sweet affection again and wishing she could look away but the truth was she couldn't. No matter how much she wanted to avoid succumbing to the growing feelings she'd been trying to ignore she simply couldn't. They were stronger than her. Persistent and unwavering as they grew with each laugh, smile, glance and touch he sent in her direction.

She was under his spell and she had never been more content with defeat. She embraced it, wrapping her arms around his neck, staring into the dark pools of blue as he pushed the boundaries of pleasure until she was teetering on that edge.

This time he didn't stop, letting her fall into the abyss. Stars exploded behind her eyes as hot waves crashed into her.

"That's right. Let go, baby." His voice sent her spiraling further. Her body racked with tremors as the pleasure continued to flow through her at unyielding speed. She didn't want it to end, but at the same time it was so intense, and she didn't know how much more her body could take.

Just as her breathing slowed, the tremors turned to mere aftershocks, Cooper got on his knees, pulling her legs up over his waist and pumped into her with unrelenting thrusts.

She tightened her legs around him, holding on for the ride. His hand came down just below her shoulder, dragging down her breasts and over her stomach before stopping at her swollen nub. He swiped his thumb across the bundle of nerves, and her body wrenched at the intense pleasure it shot through her.

He continued to rub sweet circles as he pumped into her over and over until she cried out his name, her head falling back against the pillows. He thrust one last time, his body tensing then twitching as he spilled his release.

A moment later, he collapsed beside her, his breaths coming in short jagged gasps. She found the strength to push up on her elbow and look down at him.

With a smile she said, "That was fun."

Chapter 5

Cooper laughed. Sarah's playful side that he knew was hidden beneath the aloofness had come out to play with him.

He propped himself on his elbow, mirroring her, and nodded. "Told you a little fun was good for you."

"Is that what you tell all the girls you bring up here?"

"What girls?"

"Oh please. I'm not naïve. I know your reputation."

"Not denying it, but I'm also not lying. Since I built this place I haven't had a single girl here. Other than family that is."

Her eyes widened in either shock or awe, he couldn't really tell. "Why me?"

"Why not you?"

She bit her lip, and damn if that didn't get him hard again. "That's not an answer."

He reached up, running a finger down her cheek, needing to feel her again. "There's something about you, Sarah. I just can't resist."

"I know what you mean." Her eyes dropped away, and he lifted her chin. He liked looking at her, loved how whatever she didn't say was visible in the dark round orbs of her eyes.

She was resistant to whatever this was between them, scared maybe, but he needed her to know that he was willing to try if she was. In all of his years and travels, he had never met someone like her. Someone who made him not want to quickly jump out of bed and figure out a way to get her to leave. No. He wanted her to stay. He wanted to go to sleep with her in his arms and wake up in the morning exactly the same way.

"You hungry? Thirsty?" he asked her, needing to get out of his head.

"I could go for a water."

He kissed her head and got up, moving across the small space not bothering to cover up. He loved the blush that crept up her neck when he caught her staring at his ass. Loved the way her tongue dabbed her swollen lips when she caught sight of his slowly shrinking erection. But what he really loved was the way her dark eyes lightened whenever he looked into them. How he could almost see past the carefully placed cold façade that she placed between them on that first day to the girl who just wanted to break free and have a little fun.

"One water, coming right up," he said as he made his way down the ladder.

He bent down to his mini fridge and pulled out two bottles of water. When he turned to go back, he was blessed with an amazing view of Sarah's ass coming down the ladder.

She didn't bother to cover up and while to most it wouldn't seem like a big deal after what they'd just shared, he had a feeling for Sarah, being exposed and vulnerable like this, was a very big deal. It made him think she was comfortable with him.

"Hey," he said, coming up behind her and wrapping his arms around her. He pressed the cold bottle against her breast, causing her to jump back into his chest.

He smiled, holding the bottle in front of her. "One water as promised."

"Thanks," she said, but her voice sounded distant as

she moved away from him, her eyes scouring the small space.

"What are you looking for?"

"My purse. Have you seen it?"

"Did you grab it when we left the truck?" he asked before taking a swig of water.

"Shit," she retorted.

He could almost feel the tension rolling off of her in waves.

"What's the matter?"

"My phone is in my bag and…" She took a deep breath before continuing. "I just like to have it when I'm not with Tommy in case something…"

Fully aware of her momentary freak out, Cooper stepped toward her, snaking his hand around her waist and drawing her close. He reached up, tucking her hair behind her ear. "I'm sure he's fine, but if you want I'll go get your phone." He didn't like the unease in her eyes, the tension in her shoulders. He would do anything to ease her growing worry.

She shook her head. "You know what. You're right. He's slept over with his friends before. I know the mom. He's in good hands."

"I know someone else in good hands," he said as he let his fingers slide down her bare sides to the curve of her ass. He grabbed the round globe, massaging the thick flesh and drawing her tight against him. His erection jumped back to life, pressing insistently against her stomach.

"Oh," she said as he made his intentions known and kissed her neck. "Pretty sure of yourself?"

He responded with a nip at her shoulder. She let out a startled screech that turned to laughter—better than the sounds of Sutherland Falls after a four-day trek along the Milford Track in New Zealand's South Island.

"Do I have a reason not to be?" he asked, trailing his lips down to the two perfect mounds and swirling his tongue around her nipple.

"No," she breathed.

"That's what I thought." He reached down, grabbing her ass and hoisting her up. She wrapped her legs around him as he walked them to the couch.

He sat down on the cushion, her legs straddling his hips, and dipped his head, taking her nipple back in his mouth. She tasted sweet and salty—the perfect combination.

Her fingers thrust into his hair, tugging at the strands as he grazed his teeth over the tight bud.

"Want to play a game?" he asked against her skin.

"What kind of game?"

"Truth or Dare."

"That's a kid's game."

"Not the way I play," he said with a tilt of his lips. "So truth or dare?" She didn't respond right away so he ran a finger over her hardened nipple. "Come on, Sarah, you know you want to."

"Dare," she said.

"I did not think you were a dare type of girl."

"Neither did I."

"You threw me. Now I have to think here."

"While you're thinking, truth or dare?"

"That's not how this works."

"What can I say? I'm impatient. Truth or dare?"

"Truth," he said, and she smiled. "Didn't expect that, huh?"

"I'm realizing when it comes to you I have to expect

the unexpected. So Cooper, tell me… Did you think the night would end like this?"

"I never like to be too sure of myself, and I had no expectations."

She rolled her eyes. "Right."

"No, really. I honestly wanted to go out with you, and I didn't care if we ended up back here or not. Though, I'd be lying if I said I didn't hope we would. Was this your plan all along tonight?" he asked, but she rested a finger against his mouth and shook her head.

"I believe I said dare, not truth. You're going to have to wait till my next turn."

"That's how we're going to play this?" he asked, and she nodded. "Okay then. I dare you to touch yourself."

Her eyebrows knitted together. "No."

A devilish smile spread across his face. "Yes."

"I won't."

"You have to."

She straightened her shoulders which put her tits right in front of his mouth. He couldn't help himself capturing a perfectly tight nipple between his teeth. A sexy moan rose in her throat. "I'm waiting," he said as he pulled away.

Her hand came up slowly, her fingers brushing ever so slightly against the now wet bead. Her lips parted as she traced the light brown circle, causing his cock to pulse with need. She worried her lip between her teeth, and he nearly exploded at the sight as she pinched the bud between two fingers.

He leaned back enjoying the show, resting his hands over the back of his head. She moved to the other side dragging her finger before dropping her hand to her side.

"That's it?" he exclaimed.

"You didn't say how long, so I think I more than delivered. My turn again. Truth or dare?"

"I believe it's my turn."

"Nope. You took too long to give me my dare so we skipped you, came to me, and now we're back to you. Truth or dare?"

"What do you want me to pick?" he asked, meeting her gaze.

She wiggled in his lap, and he could feel her slick heated desire. "Dare."

"Oh really? Okay then dare it is."

"I dare you to kiss me."

"That's it?"

"Here," she said, pointing down to where their bodies met.

God, if that wasn't the sexiest thing ever. In one quick motion, he had her on her back, knees bent and his head between her legs.

Before he could even taste her, there was a knock at the door, causing them both to jump back. Sarah pushed up on the couch, covering herself with her hands. Cooper looked at the clock above the sofa. "Who the hell is coming here at eleven o'clock?"

He found his t-shirt on the floor and handed it to Sarah while he grabbed a pair of gym shorts and pulled them on. Sarah quickly moved away, tugging the shirt over her head as he went to the door.

He spotted Matt outside on his porch. Confused and curious, Cooper whipped open the door. "What the hell is going on?" he asked his brother.

"Is Sarah here?"

"That's none of your business."

"Look, I'm sorry to interrupt but neither of you are answering your phones, and her son hit his head and was brought into the emergency room earlier tonight."

"What?" She pushed past Cooper and stood in front of Matt in nothing but a t-shirt, her hair a sex-rumpled mess. "Is he okay?" Panic laced her tone, and Cooper, unsure of what to do, rested a hand on her shoulder.

Matt held his hand up in a reassuring gesture. "He's fine. He fell out bed and hit his head on the dresser. Just a bump, but Gina brought him to the hospital to make sure he doesn't have a concussion. She tried calling you. I happened to be there for an unrelated accident, and she asked if I had Cooper's number, but when we couldn't get in touch with either of you."

"Oh my god. I have to go."

She went to run out the door, and Cooper grabbed her wrist. "You need to calm down first."

She ripped out of his hold. "Don't tell me what to do," she all but growled at him.

"At least put some shoes on." She looked down at her feet and pushed back into the house.

"I'm going to let you two sort this out," Matt said.

"Thanks for coming here to let us know."

"Let me know if you need me," Matt said and got back into his cruiser.

Cooper turned his attention back to Sarah who had tears in her eyes, a franticness about her that made him not want her to get behind the wheel.

"Where the hell is my other shoe?" she yelled as she tossed the pillow from the couch onto the floor. She had pulled her dress on though it was crooked and possibly on backward.

This was not how he wanted their night to end. He needed to calm her down. Needed to make her realize that her son was okay. Just a bump on the head nothing to freak out over.

"Sarah," he said, taking her hand and willing her to breathe. "You heard Matt. He's okay. They're just taking precautions."

"Okay? He's in the ER for the first time in his life, and I'm not there with him. I can't believe I didn't go get my phone. How careless and stupid."

"Gina's there. He's not alone."

"I'm his mother! *I* should be there. Not here acting like some horned up teenager. I knew this was a bad idea."

Before he could process a single thought, she found her other shoe and stormed past him in her pissed off glory. He could easily just let her go, let her cool down, but that wasn't his style. Besides there was no way in hell he was letting her drive like this.

"Hey!" he called after her as she opened the passenger door of the Jeep and grabbed her purse. He ran down the porch stairs to catch her.

"Six missed calls," she said as she shook her head in disbelief before putting the phone to her ear.

"Gina, hi it's Sarah. I'm so sorry. I'm on my way now. Can I talk to him? A CT scan? Okay. I'll be there soon. Thanks."

She hung up and bee-lined it to her car. Cooper reached out, grabbing her shoulder and managing to move in front of her. Tears glistened in her dark eyes. She was holding on but only by a thread.

"Get out of my way, Cooper."

"No," he said, needing to understand that this wasn't

her fault. He could see the guilt in her eyes and more than anything the regret. "Just because you're a mom it doesn't mean you can't have fun, that you're not entitled to take a night off. You shouldn't feel guilty about it."

"No, that's exactly what that means."

"Then you're doing it wrong."

***

Anger boiled inside of her. Every muscle in her body tensed at his words.

"You have no idea what the hell you're talking about."

"Of course I don't, because you're the only person who knows anything about parenting."

She walked closer to him, her hands twitching with the desire to smack him upside that pretty head. "And you do? The man who ran away after high school and never stayed in one place long enough to actually form a relationship with anyone? You have no idea what the hell it means to be responsible or put others before yourself. When you have a kid, come and talk to me. Until then keep your damn mouth shut."

She hopped into her car before he could stop her, slamming the door with finality. She heard her name but didn't bother looking in his direction as she floored it out of his driveway.

How could she be so stupid? So careless and irresponsible? She knew better. Tommy was the most important thing in her life, and now he was sitting in a hospital room probably scared out of his mind, and she wasn't there to comfort him.

No, she was off having sex like some floozy. Never again. This is why she didn't date. Why she didn't let loose even for a single night because no matter what Cooper believed, you didn't take a night off from being a mom. Maybe when Tommy was eighteen, but right now he was just barely seven, and he needed her more than she needed Cooper.

She pressed down on the gas a little harder but making sure to stay within ten miles of the speed limit. She'd be no good to Tommy if she was careless and lost control.

The hospital was outside of town and the drive was torturous. She wouldn't be able to breathe relief until she saw Tommy's freckle-adorned face smiling up at her.

She hopped out of her car, annoyed that she could still feel the after effects of having sex with Cooper as she moved. She ignored the sensations and hurried to the front door of the emergency room, making her way to the front desk.

"My son is here. Tommy Kramer. He hit his head. I'm his mother. He's only seven. I should've been here earlier."

The woman who had to be in her late forties met her gaze. "You're here now, sugar. That's all that matters. Now what is his name again so I can look him up in the system?"

"Tommy. Thomas Kramer."

"Here he is. Looks like he's getting ready to be released. Go through these doors right here, make a left at the first hallway, follow it down to the end, and make a right. He'll be in the first room on the left."

"Left, right, and left," she said.

"Exactly."

"Thank you. Thank you so much," she said as she hurried away from the desk and toward the door that would bring her to Tommy.

By the time she made the first left she picked up speed, moving with determined purpose. When she was at the end of the hallway she cut right and ran into the first room on the left.

As soon as her eyes settled on Tommy, the dam inside of her broke free. Tears streamed down her face as she ran to his side and wrapped him in his arms. "I'm so sorry, buddy," she said.

He wiggled in her hold, the bag of chips he was eating crinkling against her. "Mom! They gave me ice cream and told me I have a hard head."

She leaned back taking his face in her hands. "Let me look at you."

"I'm fine." He struggled against her, but she wasn't having it.

"I don't care what you say; I need to see for myself."

He rolled his eyes at her, and she chocked on a laugh as she scanned his face up and down. He had a nice welt on his forehead, and she could see the starts of a bruise, ugly swirls of yellow and blue.

She leaned in, pressing a kiss to the top of his head away from the bump. She wrapped her arms around him, hugging him tight and refusing to let go.

"Mom!" he exclaimed. "I'm okay."

She heard him but she couldn't let go. Not yet.

"Mom, you're embarrassing me."

"Get used to it," she said as she finally spotted Gina on the other side of the bed. Joey was curled up in a chair, passed out in his Spiderman pajamas. "I'm so sorry, Gina."

Gina waved her hand and shrugged. "It's no big deal. If anything, *I'm* sorry. I feel just awful about this."

"You have nothing to feel awful about."

"He got hurt at my house on my watch… Of course I do. And you had to leave your date early."

Sarah ignored the date reference, pretending like Gina never said it, mainly because she didn't want Tommy to know. "Matt said he fell out of bed. Hit his head on the dresser."

"I've been telling Chris to get rid of that stupid dresser for months. We don't even use it anymore. Just there taking up space. Tommy must've rolled out of bed. I heard him crying and came running. Once he calmed down he told me he was okay, but I wasn't taking any chances. I wanted to get him checked out just in case. I hope that's okay."

Sarah came around the bed and took Gina in a hug. "It's perfectly okay. I would have done the same thing."

"Have the doctors said anything about the CT scan?"

"They said it's just a bump. No concussion."

Relief flooded through her. "Oh thank god."

"He should be able to get out of here soon."

"You should go home. Put poor Joey to bed."

"I don't want to leave you here alone."

"It's fine. Besides, I'm not alone." She looked at her son, so happy that he wasn't seriously injured. If he had been, she would never be able to forgive herself. It was hard enough as it was.

"Okay, then I'm going to get him home," Gina bent down, all five-foot-four of her, and scooped her oversized son into her arms as if he weighed nothing. "Call me if you need anything."

"I will, and Gina, thank you so much for taking care of my boy."

"It's what we mothers do," she said and gave a bump to her shoulder as she passed.

Sarah sat down on the bed next to Tommy, kicking her feet up beside his. "I've been thinking…"

"Yeah Mom?"

"You can go to summer camp."

"What? Really!" He shot up, and she quickly reached out, holding him down.

"Be careful and yes." She had been thinking about it on and off since he had asked, and now, seeing him hurt, she felt like she needed to make up for it. Maybe it was silly, but she needed to see her son smile.

"Joey is going to be so excited. Can I call him?"

Sarah laughed. Did he not just see his best friend passed out and being carried out of the room by his mother? "Tomorrow. First thing. Promise."

"Mom?"

"Yeah, buddy?"

"Sometimes you're the coolest."

"Sometimes?" she asked with mock shock in her tone.

"Well, not when you make me clean my room and do homework."

"One day you'll appreciate it."

"No, I won't."

"Come here, you stinker." She held her arm up, and Tommy snuggled into her side. She held him close as they waited for the doctor to release him.

Chapter 6

Cooper lost track of how many times he'd called Sarah. How many texts he'd sent her. By day two of no response, he finally gave up. He tried, and just shy of going to her house, he considered it a damn good effort.

He had thought about going to her place, but there had to have been a reason she wanted to meet at his place the other night. He didn't want to piss her off any more than she already was by showing up unannounced. But what would she expect? She was leaving him hanging. He just wanted to make sure that her son was okay. That she was okay.

It was Monday, and he promised Shay he'd help out at the bakery again, so he hoped that Sarah would come in for her Monday muffin, but as the morning melted into the afternoon he finally had to accept that she wasn't going to show.

Even the sweet smell of key lime cupcakes wafting from the kitchen couldn't put him in a good mood.

Saturday night with Sarah had been unbelievably amazing, unlike anything else he'd ever experienced. She was sweet and fun. Sexy as hell, yet shy. He couldn't get the vision of her pinching her nipples out of his damn mind no matter how hard he'd tried. How her lips parted in a silent "Oh" as she allowed herself to enjoy the sensations she was triggering from her touch.

He was getting hard just thinking about it, so he forced himself to focus on the least sexy thing he could think of. He started thinking about the train ride in Bangladesh after the

EID Festival. How it was so crowded people took to the roofs of the train. He tried to get to the top and eventually made it, but the first few minutes being jam packed inside the train, sardined between people in stagnant air after a day of sweating balls was horrible to say the least.

An experience he was so honored to have been a part of but not something he'd want to do again. He could still smell the body odor of the man next to him as he lifted his arm to scratch his head.

The memory quickly erased any arousing thoughts.

The door flew open, and Cooper looked up, pathetic and hopeful, only to be disappointed by his sister Kate, poking her head in. "It's happening!" she exclaimed.

"What's happening?" he asked genuinely confused.

"The baby! Shay's water broke. Come on, you can drive with me to the hospital."

Louise came running out of the back, a smudge of flour on her brown cheek. "The baby's coming?" she asked a massive smile spreading across her face.

"He is," Kate responded, her voice going up a good five octaves.

"Oh my god! Tell Shay I'm thinking about her, and I have everything under control."

"You good if I go?" Cooper asked, not wanting to leave Louise high and dry.

"Are you kidding me? I've been preparing for this day for months. Go! Get! I got this."

"Thanks," Cooper said as he catapulted himself over the counter and joined Kate in a sprint to her car.

"Where's your husband?" he asked. Kate and Caleb had got together just around the time Cooper came home and quickly got engaged afterward. He was thrilled when one day after a two-week long vacation they came home and told everyone they had eloped. It was one less wedding he had to attend, and he couldn't have loved his sister more than in that moment.

While he loved a good party, he wasn't ready for another wedding. The last one his grandmother was all over him asking him when he planned on settling down. And though he could handle his grandma better than the rest of his siblings, he still hated to disappoint her, and that's exactly how he felt when he had told her he never planned on getting married.

Betty Hayes was usually a very understanding woman, but her desire for her grandkids to get married had taken over her common sense. With Shay pregnant, they all thought they had some time before she started her inquisition again, but if anything, it only made it worse. He could already picture her at the hospital making her rounds to each one of them while they waited.

"My husband," Kate said with a goofy smile. "God, I love saying that. My *husband*," she said again, "is bringing his car home and catching a ride with Mason so we don't have two cars at the hospital."

"Can you stop spewing your happiness? It's disgusting."

"You're just jealous."

He laughed, but the truth was, maybe a part of him, a teeny tiny part of him, was a little jealous. Kate found someone who made her ridiculously happy, yet at the same time, challenged her. Caleb embraced her ambition and knew how to rein her in when she got a little ahead of herself. It was a rare thing to find everything you need in someone else, but somehow, three of his siblings had found exactly that.

In the past, he wouldn't have given two shits about it.

But as each one of his brothers and sisters paired off, he was left wondering if he ever would—if he even *wanted* to. It was such a foreign concept for him. Falling in love, settling down with one person... he always looked at that as losing your independence. An ending to all the things he still wanted to accomplish and see in his life.

Now he wasn't so sure. And while the chemistry and attraction he had with Sarah had a lot to do with it, these doubts and uncertainties had been around much longer. They started poking at his mind as far back as Matt and Shay's wedding.

Maybe married life wasn't as bad as he had originally thought. He really had no reason to think otherwise. His parents and grandparents were happy, and that's what he'd grown up with. But he also grew up thinking that life began and ended on the farm, and he wanted more than that.

He didn't want to be mucking chicken coops for the rest of his life or designing corn mazes with Matt for Basil Hill Farms famous Fall Festival.

No, he wanted more.

The problem was no matter how many countries he had been to, how many different people he had met along the way, that craving for more never stopped. If anything, it only became greedy, growing with each new place wanting more. He kept on the move, searching for something to satisfy the desire, but nothing ever did.

Until he came home last July.

Recently he felt the desire sparking back to life, but then he met Sarah, and for the first time in his life he was content. Maybe they only had one night together, but that one night was enough to get him hooked. He needed to see her again.

"So," Kate said, and he could hear the sad attempt at trying to be nonchalant, "heard you had a hot date this weekend."

"Where'd you hear that?" he asked, not that he should be surprised. No one in his family—or this town—could keep their damn mouths shut. It was why he drove to the next town over in the first place so he and Sarah could enjoy their night without prying, noisy ass people.

"Oh, you know. Around."

"Don't play that shit with me."

"Testy are we? Matt might have mentioned it."

Cooper ran a hand through his hair, feeling the tension in his shoulders. "What'd he tell you?"

"Just that you were out with Sarah Kramer. Why? Is there more to tell?"

He rolled his eyes behind his aviators and slumped into his seat. "No."

"You're such a liar. Besides you've never been good at it, so I don't know why you even continue to try."

"Why don't you worry about driving and not worry about my dating life?"

"Because I'm a multi-tasker, and I can do both."

"I really don't want to talk about it."

"That bad, huh?"

He sat up, his palms pointing upward and resting on his knees. "No, it was fucking amazing. Then Matt knocked on my damn door, and the whole night was ruined."

Kate's eyebrows pinched together as she glanced over at him. "Why did Matt knock on your door?"

"Her kid got hurt and had to go to the emergency room. Our phones were in my truck so nobody could get in touch with us. She freaked out. Now she won't answer my damn calls, not even a freaking text message. I just want to know that she and the kid are okay."

"Oh my god," Kate said her mouth parting in that way it did when she was excited about figuring something out.

"What?"

"You like her."

"Yeah, so?"

"No. You really like her. Like, *like* her like her."

"Are you twelve? Yes, I like her. So what?"

"This is different."

"Don't read too far into this."

"I'm not, Coop. I can hear it in your voice, see it in your face. You have it bad." She laughed and shook her head with what looked like amazement. "I've never seen you like this. Ever."

"That makes two of us," he admitted.

"So what are you going to do?"

"What do you mean what am I going to do? Nothing. You heard me; she won't even take my damn calls."

"If you think making a few phone calls is all the effort the girl deserves than you don't deserve her."

"Thanks, sis."

"I'm serious. If you really want to have something with her then you need to show her that she's not just some notch on your bedpost. She needs to know you want to commit to her. That you're ready for a relationship."

"I don't know if I do. I mean, she has a kid."

"Yeah and…?"

"I don't even know if I like kids."

"Of course you like kids. You're a big kid yourself. You'll fit right in with him. Besides, Dad said you're filling in for Bob at Bob's Big Adventures."

He nodded.

"You know Bob runs the programs with the young kids, right? Not the teenagers? You'll have all summer to learn to love kids."

"Great." That would be just his luck.

Twenty minutes later, they walked into the hospital waiting room and were greeted by their parents, grandparents, and their sister Hadley.

"Any baby yet?" Cooper asked.

"She's only six centimeters dilated," his mother, Carol Hayes said.

"And that means?"

"Ideally she needs to be ten centimeters before she can start pushing."

"How long will that take?" Cooper asked, almost immediately realizing how childish he was sounding. Poor Shay was in there, having a baby wreaking havoc on her insides while she tried to bring new life into the world, and he was upset he had to wait.

"It could be a couple hours, it could be longer," Carol said, patting him on the cheek. "So find a spot and get comfy."

Cooper plopped down in a chair farthest from his grandmother, hoping the distance would deter her, and pulled out his phone. He pulled Sarah's name up and sent her another text letting her know Shay was in labor.

Maybe she would finally respond. He felt a little guilty using his sister-in-law to elicit a response, but he was desperate, and Sarah seemed to genuinely like Shay. And the way Shay tried to protect Sarah from him, he knew they were friends.

Seconds turned to minutes and eventually an hour, and

he realized that Sarah wasn't going to respond. Kate was right; Sarah deserved more than a few failed phone calls and texts, but he didn't know what else to do.

Maybe what they had was only meant to last the night. Besides, who was to say in a month or four that itch that was always hiding just beneath the surface wouldn't reappear, making him want to cut ties and head off with his backpack and passport?

After all, Shay was having the baby right now. The only reason—at least what he told himself—for sticking around was to meet his nephew. He didn't want to be the uncle his nephew only heard stories about, but that was why he wrote his book in the first place. So even if he wasn't around all the time, one day his nephew and future nieces and nephews would know who he was and where he was.

Besides, it's not like home wasn't a plane ride away. He could come back for birthdays and all that other nonsense that required a party and presents. Maybe it was time to realize that sticking around in one place was never in the cards for him.

He shoved his phone back in his pocket, accepting defeat when Betty Hayes stood from her seat and made her way toward him. Her white flowy top matched her short pixie hair. Her blue eyes focused on him, and he knew there was no way out.

She sat down in the chair next to him and patted his knee with her work worn hands. She'd been working on farms since she was a child and still helped his parents out at Basil Hill.

"What are you sulking about?" she asked.

"I'm not sulking."

She laughed loud enough to cause a few heads to turn.

"Could've fooled me. The last time I saw you looking so down in the dumps Mason had pushed you and you dropped your ice cream in the dirt."

"That was a travesty," he said with a smile.

"It was vanilla. Not much of a loss if you ask me. So tell me, does your current mood have anything to do with that sweet girl, Sarah Kramer?"

"How did you kno…?" He cut the question off before he finished it. Kate knew, so of course Betty Hayes would know. Between her and Terry at the Happy Apple it was amazing anyone in that damn town had a secret to themselves. Those two women were like vultures on roadkill the minute they thought something was up. He was pretty sure he heard Matt mentioning that Terry had a police scanner app on her phone.

He loved his grandmother to death and was fond of Terry, too, and while he would never admit it out loud, some long lonely nights he'd missed their meddling. Now that he was immersed in it he was wondering what the hell he had been thinking.

"I don't want to talk about it," he said to his grandma, but that statement was as useless as when he tried it on Kate.

"Nobody ever wants to talk about the things that are hurting them but that doesn't mean they shouldn't. I bet it'll help to get it off your chest."

"It didn't help when I talked to Kate about it."

"That's because that girl is not me. Now let me help you fix this so I can get a great grandbaby out of the deal."

"What?" Cooper shot up in his chair and looked at his grandmother like she'd lost her damn mind because she very well might have.

"Sarah already has a son. If you two are together then

that means the boy is your responsibility, too. Built-in grandson for me."

Cooper held his hand up, feeling his stomach twist in knots. "Hold up. What Sarah and I had was nothing more than one date. No one said I was signing up to be some kid's father."

"Why the heck did you go on a date with the girl… Oh!" she said, giving him a knowing smirk. "It was a sex date."

He ran his hands through his hair, seriously not wanting to have this conversation with his grandmother no less in a hospital waiting room. If the floor would open up and swallow him he'd consider himself one lucky son of a bitch.

He searched for someone to come rescue him, but Caleb, Mason, and Cassie just walked in so they were all occupied giving updates.

"It wasn't a sex date," Cooper admitted. "I genuinely wanted to go out with her. I didn't care if it ended in sex as long as we got to spend time together. It was great… until it wasn't, and maybe it was a blessing in disguise. I'm not capable of being some sort of father figure. Like Kate said, I'm still a kid myself."

"You my boy do not give yourself enough credit."

"Grandma let's be serious."

"Oh I am. I helped raise you, so if you think you're not capable then that makes me a failure."

"I know what you're doing," he said, meeting Betty's blue eyes. "And guilt tripping isn't going to work this time."

"Darn." She snapped her fingers. "I must be getting rusty in my old age."

"Or I'm getting wiser in mine."

She patted his knee. "No dear. I don't think so." Her

face was stone cold, and Cooper looked at her in shock until she burst out laughing. "Not as rusty as I thought."

Cooper laughed with her, and it felt good after his shitty weekend.

"Do yourself a favor," she said, taking his hand in hers. "Do what you always do and follow your heart. It hasn't steered you wrong yet."

Betty Hayes was at times inappropriate and always wedging her nose where it didn't belong, but she also gave some of the best advice.

"Thanks, Grandma," Cooper said.

"Anytime, dear. Now excuse me. I have to go ask your sister when she plans on getting knocked up."

Cooper smiled as his grandmother walked across the waiting room and cornered Kate and Caleb. Kate threw him a pleading look, but he just shook his head and laughed. She didn't come to his rescue a few seconds ago, so she was on her own. Besides, she had her husband to help defend her against Betty.

"Did we miss it?" Hadley came into the waiting room with Matt's best friend and local fire chief, Sam Bennett.

"Not yet," Jonathon Hayes said as he stood up to give Sam a proper handshake. "Did you two come together?" he asked, eyeing them both curiously.

"No, we just happened to see each other in the parking lot," Sam answered before greeting the rest of the clan.

He and Hadley plopped in open seats in the corner and joined the rest of the family.

The clock on the wall seemed to be moving at a snail's pace.

Cooper was getting antsy. It had only been two hours, and he was tempted to go home and have them call him when the baby arrived, but then he saw Mason drumming his fingers on his knees. He didn't do well in hospitals, and even though Cassie was sweetly rubbing his arm, it only seemed to help a little.

"You okay, Mace?" Cooper asked.

He looked down at his moving fingers and quickly flattened his hands, rubbing them against the knees of his jeans. "Fine," he answered.

Cooper was about to ask him about his newest batch of pale ale when Matt came flying into the room.

"Saved by the baby," Kate mumbled as Betty and everyone turned to Matt with bated breath.

"He's here!" he announced, and the entire half of the waiting room that they overtook erupted into excited cheers. "Seven pounds, eight ounces and healthy as can be."

"That's because he's a Hayes," Harold Hayes said with a nod of approval.

"Always has to take credit," Betty murmured.

"Time to celebrate." Jonathon Hayes reached into the inside pocket of his jacket and pulled out a bunch of cigars, handing one to Matt.

"How's Shay?" Mason asked.

"Good," Matt said with a smile. "My girl is a fucking champ."

Carol Hayes pointed her finger at Matt. "Mouth." That typical Mom tone they were all used to caused all of them to laugh. No matter how old they got, how many kids they had, it didn't matter to their mother. In her eyes, they were still her babies.

Matt wrapped their mom in a huge hug, kissing her on the head before pulling away. "I have to get back to Shay. They'll be putting the baby in the nursery soon. If you come out in the hallway they said they'll wheel him by so you all can get a good look."

"Get out of my way," Betty Hayes said, pushing her way to the door. "I need to see my great grandbaby." As she passed Matt she reached up and stood on tiptoes, pinching his cheek. "You made me proud."

A genuine smile spread across Matt's face before he kissed his grandma's cheek. "Shay needs to rest so if it's all right by you, no visitors tonight."

Everyone gave a collective nod, knowing even if they didn't agree, when it came to his wife there was absolutely no arguing.

"I love you guys," Matt said before hurrying back to Shay.

The family gathered in the hallway, waiting for the new edition to the family to make his grand entrance.

A nurse came into view, pushing a hospital bassinet toward them. "Are you the Hayes family?" she asked as she approached, making it clear that they weren't in Red Maple Falls.

"Yes," they answered in unison.

"Here's your new edition: Matthew Jonathon Hayes Junior."

Betty clapped her hands together, tears glistening in her eyes as she gazed down upon her first great-grandbaby. After all these years of pestering and hoping, her wish was finally granted. She was a great-grandmother.

Everyone took turns looking down at the red-faced nugget like he was a trophy on display. He was the newest generation of Hayes, and if the poor kid knew what he was getting himself into, he might've climbed back into the womb.

One thing was for certain. He would be loved.

Cooper moved closer, looking down at his nephew. He didn't expect to feel much of anything so when warmth filled him, pure joy racing through his body causing him to smile uncontrollably, he knew that this kid, not even a few hours old, did something that no one else had been able to do.

He gave Cooper a reason to want to stay.

Chapter 7

The phone calls and texts stopped, but that didn't keep Sarah from checking her phone every now and again. Her heart sunk a little at the lack of new messages. It was what she wanted, which was why she never answered, so why did it hurt so much that he gave up on her?

She was being ridiculous, and she knew it, which was exactly why she hadn't been by Shay's house to congratulate her and bring a little something for the baby and the new mom-to-be. She had bought the gift over a month ago in anticipation for the day, and the gift bag had been sitting on her dresser for a week, taunting her.

Everyone in Red Maple Falls was talking about the new baby, and it was time Sarah sucked it up and went over there. She waited until the middle of the morning when she assumed Cooper would either be helping out at the bakery or out on his parents' farm. Who knew, maybe he'd even still be sleeping since he didn't have any real responsibilities. Or possibly flew off to some faraway country because it's what he did.

She mentally scolded herself. It wasn't his fault she got knocked up at eighteen. He had every right to live the way he wanted to, and she shouldn't judge him. It just pissed her off that he had the nerve to tell her that she was parenting wrong. Who the hell did he think he was? If they were discussing ethnic cuisine or airfare from one country to the next he'd have a leg to stand on because that was his thing. Parenting was hers. She was a mom, and a darn good one, dammit. He had no right to judge her.

She took a deep breath, letting the anger subside as she grabbed the baby blue gift bag off of her dresser, ignoring how the color reminded her of Cooper's eyes, and headed for the car.

If she didn't go now she never would, and that wasn't who she was. She was the person who showed up with flowers the minute someone was having a bad day. The person who had a gift for every occasion, handpicked and perfectly suited to the person. Like being a mother, it was who she was, what she was good at.

Ten minutes later, she pulled into Shay and Matt's driveway and parked next to Shay's new Audi wagon. Sarah laughed, thinking about the day she walked into the bakery to order her usual muffin when Shay was on a war path because Matt wanted her to buy a minivan. It was as if the man didn't know his wife at all.

A girl who was born and raised in New York City, a place of style, did not want to be driving all over the town in an oversized fam van. Shay had slammed Sarah's muffin down on the counter in disgust, and that's when Sarah had suggested the all-wheel drive station wagon.

Luckily for Matt, Shay liked the idea, and luckily for Shay, Matt did, too.

Sarah walked up the path to the log cabin on the lake and knocked on the door, wishing she would have called first or at least sent a text. She hated arriving unexpectedly.

Matt opened the door with a smile, and the tension in her shoulders eased, but she could see the bags beneath his eyes, the messy spikes of his hair, and the stain on his shirt—the sure signs of a baby who doesn't like to sleep.

"Hi, Sarah. What a nice surprise," he said as he

motioned for her to come inside. "Come in."

She walked into the beautiful home that managed to capture both Matt and Shay's style of rustic and chic. "You look like you need a nap," she said with a sympathetic smile.

"I've been trying to let Shay sleep as much as she can before I have to go back into work next week."

Sarah remembered the awful middle of the night feedings, the constant crying that seemed to go on for days, how her mom offered to help in the beginning, but she was so determined to do it all on her own. It wasn't until she broke down into tears herself when her mom took Tommy and sent her to bed. She must have slept for twelve hours straight that night.

While she loved her son more than anything in the world, she had no desire to have another baby. And if for whatever reason she decided she did, she was never doing it alone. She'd have a partner to help her.

"That's really sweet of you, and I'm sure it means so much to Shay."

He shrugged. "It's the least I can do. She carried him around for nine months then was in labor for six hours. A few nights of missed sleep is nothing compared to that."

"Are there more of you out there?" she joked.

He smiled that Hayes charm evident even through the exhaustion. "I am the best, but I do have brothers."

Realizing the massive hole she'd just stepped in, she tried her best to recuperate. "Forget I said that."

"Speaking of brothers," he said, but the last thing she wanted was to talk to Matt about Cooper. If anything, she just wanted to forget that night ever happened. It was for the best.

She waved her hand, but before she could get any

words out she heard the distinct sound of Cooper's voice coming into the living room. "Matt, Shay needs some Desitin. She said you'd know what I'm talking about."

"Yup. Excuse me. I'll be right back," Matt said

The minute Cooper looked up from his phone and his eyes met hers, she felt the air suck out of the room. He froze on spot, an unreadable expression on his face.

"Sarah," he said, sounding almost as shocked as she felt. "What are you doing here?"

She held up the gift bag and tried to pretend like seeing him didn't tear a hole in her chest. "I'm bringing Shay and the baby a gift. What are you doing here? I mean… Your truck wasn't outside."

He ran a hand over his head, resting it on the back of his neck. "I rode my bike."

"Here it is," Matt said, coming back into the room.

Cooper went to reach for it, but Sarah stepped in front of him. "I'll take it to Shay. I want to give her this anyway." She held up the gift bag and smiled at Matt.

"She's in the nursery. Down the hall, third door on the right," he said.

Sarah hurried away, refusing to even look at Cooper because she knew the minute she did every memory from their night together would flood into her. She'd finally accepted what she had known all along—Cooper Hayes and her could never work. She was focused on her son and her career, and he was focused on…Well, she wasn't even sure, but it definitely wasn't a steady relationship.

At the third door, Sarah peeked in, lightly knocking on the door.

Shay, who was standing by the window holding her newborn, danced to a silent song. Bubbles, their adorable adopted dog with a white face and brown head sat at her feet. When she heard the knock, she spun around.

"Sarah!" she said with a big smile. She was absolutely glowing as she held her son closely to her chest. Bubbles sat up and nudged Shay's leg.

"It's okay, Bubbles," Shay said, bending down and patting the dogs head. "He's been overly protective of the baby. It's super sweet." She motioned to Sarah. "Come in. Come in."

Sarah gave Shay a hug. "Congratulations, Mommy. How are you feeling?"

"Surprisingly well."

Shay pulled the blanket away from the baby, and Sarah looked down at the angelic face. "He's beautiful."

"Thank you. Do you want to hold him?"

"Of course!" She lifted her arm, realizing she was still holding the present. "I got you both a little something," Sarah said, placing the bag on the changing table.

"You didn't have to."

She waved her hand at Shay. "Please. Now give me that adorable baby boy."

"Just a warning, he tends to get a bit fussy with other people." Shay handed little Matthew over to her, and she rested her hand behind his head for support. His little hands moved, little feet fidgeted as he got comfortable to his new space. Sarah rocked him gently, cooing down at him until he relaxed into her arms.

"You're a pro," Shay said.

"I've had some practice. God, it's been seven years, but you never forget."

"Do you want more?" Shay asked, causing Sarah to freeze for a moment before continuing to rock Matthew.

"I don't think so. It's been me and Tommy for so long. I can't imagine anything else."

"Two years ago, I wouldn't have imagined reconnecting with Matt, falling in love all over, getting married and having a baby, but here I am."

"You two are different."

"How?"

"You guys were written in the stars."

Shay rolled her eyes then laughed. "That's a load of crap. We just got under each other's skin and never fully recovered."

Sarah thought of Cooper who was only a few doors away. How, ever since their date, she couldn't get him off her mind. How every damn thing reminded her of him. How she couldn't even think about his lips on her without having aftershocks ravage her body.

The night was perfect... until it wasn't, and she had to remind herself over and over that everything happened for a reason. Tommy getting hurt was a reminder that her main focus in life was her son. She couldn't let anyone take his place or let her for a minute not be there for him a hundred and ten percent like she had been all along.

She was fine with that notion for so long, but Cooper, like Shay had said, got under her skin. She wondered how long he would be there. If it was only a momentary blip in time or if he would always be there, reminding her of how happiness could only lead to heartbreak. How letting loose and having fun had consequences.

The baby let out a content sigh and opened his eyes, shocking her with the intense blue. They were just like his uncle's, and it made Sarah think things she shouldn't.

She ignored the idea of a baby Cooper and wondered

about the baby in her arms. Would his eyes stay this color or change to be green like his father's or hazel like his mother's? Either way he would be gorgeous. He had good genes.

Sarah felt his presence before she heard him or saw him. In a moment of weakness, she looked up, and he caught her gaze. He stared at her unnervingly as she held his nephew in her arms. He swallowed, his Adam's apple rising and falling.

The urge to flee consumed her as she turned to Shay. "I should get going." She handed the baby back and gave Shay a kiss on the cheek. "Call me if you need anything."

A little stunned by Sarah's sudden departure, Shay stuttered before settling for a nod.

"I will and thanks," Shay finally called after her, but Sarah was almost at the door. She kept her head down as she pushed past Cooper, hoping like hell she could make a clean break. She got into the hallway and picked up speed. Matt called a goodbye after her, and she waved over her shoulder.

She managed to get to the door and was about to sigh in relief when she heard footsteps behind her.

"Sarah, wait! Please?"

Her body betrayed her, freezing in place. She wanted to run out of there and not look back but she couldn't get her legs to cooperate. He came up behind her, that delicious manly scent of citrus and woods surrounding her. She could feel the heat from his body as he placed a hand on her arm.

It was gentle and sweet, making it really hard for her to keep her resolve. "Talk to me," he said, his body coming closer to her. His chest bumped against her back with each breath he took.

She swallowed, trying to find the courage to face him.

"I just want to know that you're okay."

She took a deep breath and turned, forcing herself to keep any and all emotion from her face when she met his beautiful blue eyes. "I'm fine."

"I don't like how we left things."

"You mean when you told me that I'm a bad mother?"

"Those words never came out of my mouth. I would never say that or think that."

"No, but that doesn't stop you from thinking I'm doing it wrong." Her eyes narrowed on him as she waited for his answer. It didn't matter what he said; she had already made up her mind.

"I didn't mean it like that. It came out all wrong."

"So, what exactly did you mean?"

He ran a hand through his hair, frustration obvious in the strain of his veins, the stubborn set of his jaw. "God, Sarah why are you making this so hard? I don't know exactly what I meant. All I know is that I couldn't stand to see the guilt in your eyes. To see one silly thing ruin everything we had that night."

"Silly thing? My son getting hurt is not just some 'silly thing.'"

"Dammit! Stop twisting my words around."

"You're doing a damn good job of it yourself."

"So, that's it, then? You're just going to act like that night meant nothing to you."

"It didn't," she said, but even she could detect the pathetic attempt at keeping her voice steady.

"That's a damn shame. Because it meant something to me, and despite the way it ended, I'll always remember it as being one of the best nights of my life."

Her resolve was breaking, hot pathetic tears pressed against the back of her eyes. She was on the verge of falling apart, but before she did Cooper looked at her long and hard then walked away.

Her heart and her head battled it out. As she reminded herself it was for the best, it took everything she had not to run after him, but in the end, she walked away, too.

But instead of feeling a sense of closure like she had hoped, all she felt was empty.

Chapter 8

He tried and he failed. Honestly, what else could he do at this point? She could barely even look at him. It was as if she was a completely different person from the woman he spent one of the best nights of his life with. He hadn't been lying when he'd told her that. He needed her to know. She wasn't just another girl he messed around with; she meant something.

Clearly, he didn't mean anything to her or she would remove that stick she had wedged so far up her ass and give him another chance. But no, all she cared about was twisting his damn words around and making him sound like some insensitive asshole when that was the farthest thing from who he was.

So what if only a few days prior he decided it was for the best for them to go their separate ways? She had a kid, and he had no idea how much longer he was going to stick around; honestly it was for the best. But when he walked into Matt and Shay's living room and saw her standing there, long black hair falling in soft waves over her shoulders, those dark brown eyes landing on him, every reason of why they could never work vanished. All he wanted was to talk to her, hold her and hear that sexy as hell laugh that made him hard at the thought.

"Want to talk about it?" Matt asked as Cooper passed him and headed to the back door.

"No, I don't want to fucking talk about it."

"That's it. I'm getting a swear jar. I don't want my kid's

first word to be 'fuck.'" Shay slapped a hand over her mouth and looked down at little Matthew. "That's a bad word. We don't say those. Coop, I'll let it slide this time. Next time, five bucks."

Cooper reached into his pocket and pulled out a twenty, handing it to Shay. "Consider it an advance," he said.

She took the money without question and turned to Matt. "We might be able to pay for Matthew's college this way."

"Between you and me we'll be broke in a week and tapping into the jar to take our money back."

Shay gave a noncommittal shrug then moved her attention to Cooper who was about to head outside.

"You okay?" she asked.

"Just dandy."

He opened the door then shut it before going out. "You'd think that *I* was the one who hurt her son," he blurted as he spun toward Matt and Shay. "Like it's my fucking fault the kid fell out of bed and hit his head."

Shay held up a finger. "That's one for the swear jar."

Cooper ignored her, too consumed in his own thoughts.

"She acted like a kid's never got hurt before. Like I'm the bad guy in this fucking scenario. Yeah, I know that's two," he said to Shay before continuing. "I tried calling her after. Sent a thousand texts to see how she and the kid were and she blew me off. Like what we had meant fucking nothing to her."

"Did it mean something to you?" Shay asked, her eyebrow arching.

He paused. "All I know is I like her. I had fun, and I know damn well she did, too up until this asshole knocked on my fucking door and ruined everything." Cooper reached into his pocket and pulled out another twenty, slapping it into Shay's palm.

"Hey," Matt said, holding his hands up. "I couldn't just sit there knowing she might be with you and *not* do something. Her kid was hurt for crying out loud."

"I know! But it still fucking sucks that's how our night ended. And now I might as well have the damn plague because she can't even stand to be in the same room with me."

"I doubt it has anything to do with you," Shay offered. "Sarah's been coming into my bakery since I opened. She was actually one of my first customers. Her son is her world. So much so that it took us almost two years before we went from store owner and customer to friends. She doesn't put herself first; everything she does is for her kid. The fact that she even agreed to go out with you says something. Maybe right now your timing is off, but if you really like her then give her some time to cool off, reminisce a little, and maybe she'll come around."

Cooper scoffed. "And maybe pigs will fly."

"You have to have a little more faith than that."

"What do you think?" Cooper asked Matt who had been leaning against the counter and silently observing.

"My wife is always right."

Shay let out a loud barking laugh. "Since when?"

"Since I'm trying to earn brownie points for when the doctor gives you clearance."

"Because you want some of this," Shay motioned to her body. "I smell like spit up, I haven't washed my hair in three days, and those damn celebrities make you think you'll lose the baby weight right away, but nope. It's still here."

Matt walked toward her, taking her in his arms. "You're beautiful."

"And that's my cue to leave," Cooper said, feeling incredibly uncomfortable.

"Like you've never seen a man be affectionate to his wife before," Shay said with a laugh. "Don't forget I know your parents and your grandparents really well. You grew up with this shit."

"Swear jar," Matt said without skipping a beat.

"Damn it!"

"Again."

"Whose stupid idea was this?" Shay asked with a roll of her eyes.

Matt and Cooper looked at each other, then at Shay. "Yours," they said in unison.

"I'll put my money in the pot later. I'm going to go put him down. Not a peep from either of you."

"We'll be out on the deck. Call me if you need me," Matt said before giving Shay a kiss.

"Coop, if it's any consolation, I take back what I said a couple weeks ago."

"What'd you say?" Matt asked, but Shay ignored him, keeping her eyes on Cooper.

"You are her type, and while I haven't spoken to either of you about the other, I can see it in both of your eyes. I think it's something worth fighting for and, in this case, waiting for. Now get out of my house."

Cooper walked over to Shay, took her into a sideways embrace, and kissed the top of her head. "Thanks," he said before following his brother out to the deck.

Matt held up his phone. "Mason just texted. He's on his way. I told him to bring beer."

"Perfect," he said and sat down on the Adirondack chair facing the lake.

If Cooper had to wait, there was no better way to spend his time than enjoying the beautiful day while drinking some beer with his brothers.

***

Sarah had a custom order she needed to complete and ship out, but how the hell was she supposed to concentrate when all she could think about was what Cooper had said.

I'll always remember it as being one of the best nights of my life.

Did he actually mean it? The man had travelled all over the world, met hundreds, probably *thousands* of people, experienced things people couldn't even fathom, yet a night with her in the middle of nowheresville was one of the best nights of his life?

It had to have been a line, some bullshit to try and make himself feel better about the other things he had said that she may or may not have misconstrued.

"Just let it go," she said out loud as she hunched forward in her chair and picked up a pair of bending pliers. She tried to focus on the piece in front of her, but his damn words were stuck on repeat and wouldn't go away no matter how hard she tried to ignore them.

Finally, with her patience spent, she tossed the tool onto the table and slumped back into her chair. "Damn it," she muttered just as the sadness she had been ignoring pushed to the surface.

She hated to cry. Ever since Tommy's sperm donor left her in a pile of her own tears for a week, she vowed to herself that she'd never give another man that sort of power over her. She wouldn't give *anyone* that sort of power, and here she was, seven years later, trying so hard not to cry when really all she wanted to do was fall apart.

Maybe if she gave herself this tiny moment of weakness, she'd finally be able to get back to business. It's not like Tommy was home; he was at school, and he'd never know. By the time she picked him up, she'd be fine.

So she took a deep breath and let free the emotion that had been consuming her since she heard Cooper's voice at Shay's.

The first tear dropped then it was like the Hoover Dam let loose as tears flowed down her cheeks in record breaking streams. "You're so pathetic," she said to herself as she grabbed a tissue from the box she kept on a side table by her desk and bloated at the mess.

Just as she was about to spiral into a black hole of self-deprecation, her cell phone rang. She swiped at the tears and grabbed for the phone, confused to see a strange area code. She thought about ignoring it, but just in case it was a business call she cleared her throat and answered, trying her best not to sound like she was just crying like a baby.

"Hi Sarah, this is Bex Shepard."

Her eyes widened, and she flung straight up in her chair, practically dropping the phone in the process.

"Bex Shepard," she managed.

"Do you remember me?"

Was she kidding? Bex Shepard was the reason she had a career.

"Of course, of course. How are you?"

"Fantastic. I'm actually preparing to leave for Cannes in a couple weeks and was hoping to wear one of your pieces."

Sarah couldn't even form a coherent thought. Bex Shepard wanted to wear one of her pieces at Cannes Film Festival where the fashion is just as important as the films being honored. This couldn't be real. She had to be dreaming or hallucinating. Maybe all that crying had gone to her head.

"I can send you pictures of my dresses, and we can see what you come up with."

Sarah sat there in stunned silence.

"Oh no, is it too late? Maybe you have something lying around that'll match my dresses."

"No!" she finally managed. "I mean. It's not too late. Not at all." She would stay up all night every night if it meant getting Bex Shepard to wear something of hers at Cannes Film Festival. This was an opportunity of a lifetime. People prayed for a big break like this, and it never happened, yet somehow for Sarah it fell into her lap. She'd be a fool not to take advantage of this opportunity.

"Send me the pictures. Email or text, and I will send some ideas and concepts back in the next forty-eight hours."

"Oh, that's wonderful! Thank you so much, Sarah."

"No, thank you. It's an honor to work with you."

"You say that now," Bex said with a laugh. "We'll see how you feel in a couple weeks when I get Cannes crazy."

"I have a seven-year-old son. Not much can scare me off."

Bex laughed. "Good to know. I'll have my assistant send those pictures right over to you."

"Sounds perfect."

"Great. I'll be in touch."

The line went dead, and Sarah placed her phone on her work table, staring at in shock when the realization finally settled in. She let out a scream of joy and fist pumped the air with both fists.

She couldn't believe how her awful day just did a

complete and total one-eighty. She had so much to do. She needed to call Ellie and see if she had anything new in the shop. Then she needed to go to the craft store a few towns over and pick up a few pieces since she didn't have time to order them online.

With a million thoughts running through her head, she grabbed her planner and started jotting down notes and creating a timeline.

Things with Cooper might not have gone the way she had hoped, but at least now she had something to occupy her mind for the next few weeks. Besides, this was going to take all of her attention outside of Tommy, so really, everything happened exactly how it should have.

She never questioned the universe before, and this just reinforced why she shouldn't. Everything that happened did so for a reason.

She didn't have time to date. Not now, when so much was riding on her to deliver.

More good things were about to happen, and the last thing she needed was a distraction like Cooper Hayes.

Chapter 9

Forgotten Treasures was a free-standing building a few miles off Main Street toward the north end of town. The wraparound porch that led up to the old building that looked like a cross between a house and a barn was decorated with old bicycles and rocking chairs. A large sign with the word *Antiques* hung above the door, while potted plants lined the stairs.

This store was one of Sarah's favorite places. She could easily get lost for hours, scouring the shelves and digging through the boxes in the back that hadn't yet been shelved and Ellie gave her special access to.

The scent of old wood and dusty tapestries mixed with apple cinnamon potpourri surrounded her as she opened the door and stepped inside.

Sarah glanced at all the new pieces as she made her way to the counter where Ellie kept all the jewelry.

"I'll be right with you," she heard Ellie call from the back.

Sarah looked at the necklaces hanging from the old rustic rake that was mounted on the wall, picking a few that she knew she could use for other pieces.

Even though Sarah had Bex's dresses marked to memory she slipped out her phone with the pictures anyway. It had gone from one piece to one for each dress. Now she had three pieces to custom make in two weeks.

The first dress was a beautiful one strap coral chiffon with a slit in the front. The second a vibrant bright baby blue that would look amazing paired with a blue spinel gemstone incrusted piece. She tried not to think about how that color reminded her of Cooper and swiped to the next picture of a to-die-for sea foam green dress encrusted with Swarovski crystals around the bodice. The dress had built in jewelry so she knew she wanted to go simple. Maybe a killer bracelet to complement it, or a pair of chandelier earrings.

She put the phone on the counter and looked through the glass case at the new pieces that came in within the past couple of days.

"Sorry about that. How can I... oh it's just you," Ellie said with a wave of her hand.

Sarah laughed. "Just me"

Ellie and Sophie were twins but couldn't be more different. While Sophie dressed like she just walked off an Ann Taylor runway in her perfectly tailored dress pants with adorable tops and matching cardigans, Ellie was more casual, opting for long Bohemian dresses or skinny jeans and flowy tops. Sophie also kept their natural blonde while Ellie dyed hers to bring out the red.

Ellie walked over and gave Sarah a hug hello. "Let me show you that piece I told you about over the phone. I hid it behind the counter just for you."

"That makes a girl feel special."

"It should."

Ellie pulled out a stunning Bohemian garnet rosette fringe necklace set in light gold. "Wow this is gorgeous."

"I found it at an estate sale down in Mass over the weekend."

Sarah picked it up and admired the craftsmanship. The rubies were fake, but it didn't make the piece any less beautiful. Besides, costume jewelry was meant to dazzle, and this necklace did exactly that. "It would be a shame to take it apart."

"Maybe, but think of what you can make from it if you did."

The gears in Sarah's head started to turn. Idea after idea sparked to life and convinced her that she had to have it. "Bag it up."

"That's what I thought."

"Now I'm looking for something with turquoise in it. It could be beads or stones."

"I have a few pieces over here." Ellie moved to the other side of the counter and took out a display case with exactly what Sarah was looking for.

"Perfect." She picked up two necklaces and a bracelet. "I'll take these three as well."

"I love when you're in spending mode," Ellie said with a smile.

"Me too. My pockets don't, but who cares about them?"

"You'll make it all back once you sell whatever master piece you're going to create."

"Hopefully."

"Oh please. You know you will."

The bell above the door chimed, and Ellie looked up to greet the customer. "Hey, Cooper," she said, and Sarah's heart plummeted to her stomach.

What the hell was he doing here? She understood bumping into him at Shay and Matt's house, but this was *her* happy place, not his. What business could he possibly have here? Unless he and Ellie had something going on. No. He wouldn't have moved on so quickly. Would he?

"Hey Ellie," he said, walking over to the counter. He

came to a stop next to Sarah, surrounding her in his distinct scent that made her mouth water. "Sarah."

"Cooper."

"You two know each other?"

"No," Sarah said when Cooper said, "Yes."

They both turned and looked at each other, Sarah trying to will him to keep his mouth shut about whatever it was that had transpired between the two of them. She didn't need the whole world knowing about her personal life even if Ellie would eventually find out. After all, she was Sophie's twin sister and also her good friend.

Mainly she wasn't ready to answer questions about that night because she still couldn't seem to understand it all.

"Okay then," Ellie said.

"I mean. We know each other through Shay," Sarah finally said, hoping that would satisfy all.

"How are they doing? Her and the baby?"

Saved by the baby.

"Great," Cooper answered. "Matt's back at work, so the whole family takes turns stopping in throughout the day to check on them. I think Shay wants to kill us all, but Matt insists."

"I'm sure she appreciates the help even if it doesn't seem like it right now," Ellie said.

"Well, if I go missing, check her trunk."

"Duly noted. Now let me go in the back and get that piece for you."

Ellie disappeared into the back storage area, and an awkward silence settled between the two.

He crossed his arms and rested his back against the display case, his biceps pressing dangerously hard against the thin material of his t-shirt.

"Are you stalking me?" she blurted.

"Don't flatter yourself, baby."

"Don't call me that."

"It didn't seem to be a problem a couple weeks ago when I was inside you."

Sarah sucked in a shocked breath, her eyes narrowing on this crude man who annoyed her in the worst way, yet still managed to turn her on. It was a damn mystery how he elicited two very different emotions inside her.

"A bit inappropriate, don't you think?"

"Me?" He pointed to his chest in mock surprise. "The man who has no idea what the hell it means to be responsible or put others before myself? No. That doesn't seem right."

He threw her own words back in her face just like she had done to him time and again, but now she understood how badly it hurt. She didn't mean what she said. Not really. Maybe she could have phrased it better or not said it at all.

While the words hurt her to hear them, she could see that they hurt him, too, and that was far worse. In the heat of the moment she wanted to hit him hard, but now seeing the wounded expression in his eyes she felt bad. Really bad.

"I'm sorry I said that."

"I'm not."

She glanced up in confusion. "You're not?"

"No, because it told me how you really feel."

"Cooper, that's not—"

"It's okay. I get it and it's fine. Just means that I have to find a way to prove you wrong."

"Prove me—"

"Here it is!" Ellie announced as she walked back up front holding the vintage wooden beer case. "The writing is fading just a little bit over here." She pointed to a small spot on the right. "But other than that this thing is in great condition. I think it'll match the décor of the brewery perfectly."

Cooper took the piece from Ellie and gave it a once over. "This is great. I think Mace will love it. You still have my card on file?"

"I do."

"Go ahead and charge it."

"What's it for?" Sarah asked. She knew it was none of her business, and if Cooper told her exactly that, she would understand completely.

"Have you been to Five Leaf?" Cooper asked, referring to his brother's brewery that opened that past fall. Sarah didn't drink often, and when she did, she always preferred a glass of white wine.

"I haven't," she admitted. "But I've heard great things." After the grand opening, she couldn't go many places without someone talking about how much they enjoyed the brewery and how Mason had outdone himself.

"Then you wouldn't know, but the décor consists of a mix of vintage beer memorabilia and pieces that have history here in Red Maple Falls. Mason has been busy keeping up with the demand, so I've been working with Ellie to get a few more pieces to add to the space."

"That's really nice of you to help him out like that."

"He's my brother. Besides, I have the time. It would be selfish of me not to offer."

She cut her eyes to him. He might not have come right out and said it, but she knew what he was getting at. He was inadvertently throwing her words back in her face again. If that's how he wanted to act then two could play that game.

"While this has been fun, I really need to get back to work. Unless this wasn't fun, and I'm just doing it wrong. I have no idea. What is fun exactly?"

This time Cooper's eyes narrowed on her then an insinuating eyebrow arching in her direction. There gazes met in a clash of heated exasperation, neither budging to break free first.

"Did I miss something?" Ellie asked.

"No," they said in unison.

"Oh, I totally did."

Out of the corner of her eye, Sarah watched Ellie clap to herself before leaving them alone to continue their battle of... well, she had no idea what exactly it was they were doing other than acting like petulant children.

She broke her gaze. "I don't have time for this. I have three pieces I have to make and have ready to be on a plane to Cannes with Bex Shepard in two weeks."

His eyes softened as he stared at her with that sweet smile that made her heart hurt. "Bex Shepard commissioned you for more pieces?"

She tucked her hair behind her ear, uncomfortable at the sudden change in the awed way he was looking at her. "Yes."

"Congratulations. That's amazing."

She shifted from one foot to the other. "Thanks."

Cooper waved goodbye to Ellie then turned back to Sarah and winked. "Just don't forget about us little people when you become some famous jewelry designer for the stars," he said before walking out the door.

Impossible, Sarah thought. *Impossible.*

Chapter 10

Cooper was excited for his first day at Bob's Big Adventures. He had several meetings with Bob himself to go over protocol and the itineraries Bob had already mapped out for the summer program. He told Cooper as long as he followed the day's activities he could infuse whatever other lessons he wanted to into the day.

Usually one to go with the flow, Cooper opted to actually review the itineraries and see how he could put his own spin on each one. Maybe it was self-preservation as he tried to forget about Sarah and that feisty attitude of hers. The way her teeth slid over her lip when she knew she was being mean. Or how her eyes dropped from his when she became uncomfortable with their conversation.

He had taken Shay's advice and stepped back. He stopped texting, calling… and ever since that accidental bump in at Forgotten Treasures he hadn't seen her. He heard from the town gossip circuit that the commissioned pieces she made for Bex Shepard were a huge success and had made it into several publications and even became a hot topic of discussion on some fashion show that exclusively discussed red carpet fashion.

There were so many times when he wanted to send her a text, congratulating her on her victory, but he'd thought better of it. One day—and he was confident that day would come—he would see her face to face and tell her in person.

Maybe when she came around she would be comfortable with introducing him to her son. After spending time with his nephew, the whole concept of kids was growing on him. Matt was such a hard ass, but the minute his son was mentioned or he was anywhere near his vicinity the big guy turned to a teddy bear. And while in the past Cooper would have bashed on him, something in him understood it, respected it, and maybe even envied it a little.

Cooper grabbed his clipboard and headed out of the main office to where other staff members were organizing the kids and getting them into their assigned groups. He found his group at the far left.

"Hey guys," Cooper said to the ten pairs of eyes staring back at him.

He heard a tiny throat clear and felt an insistent tap on his arm. He turned to see no one then looked down.

His eyes caught that of an adorable blonde girl with big brown eyes. "And lady," she said, planting her hands on her hips.

"I'm sorry. Hey guys and lady."

"Better," she said, taking her spot in the front.

"Why is there a girl here?" A tall boy with pudgy cheeks asked. "This is boys only."

"Now wait a minute," Cooper said holding his hand up, hoping to buy himself some time to think of a response. He wasn't equipped for this. Kayaking, hiking, rock climbing, yes. Boys who still thought girls had cooties? Not so much.

A kid with brown hair and a sprinkling of freckles pushed his way to the front and stood beside Cooper, his arms crossing over his small chest. "Come on, girls can join if they want."

"Shut up, Tommy. Nobody asked you."

Cooper gave the kid credit for trying. He went to walk away, and Cooper rested his hand on his shoulder. "Tommy, is it?" He looked down at the boy who looked up with big brown eyes and nodded. "Tommy is right. She has as much right to be here as you do, and if you don't like it, you don't have to come anymore. See this is my group, and it is my rules, and I say the more the merrier."

The pudgy cheeked kid rolled his eyes, probably not used to not getting his way. If he actually showed up again, Cooper hoped he could teach the kid some basic manners.

"I want you all to follow this path, and when you get to the clearing take a seat on one of the wooden seats. Tommy?"

"Yes, sir?"

"Call me Cooper. That goes for all of you. My name is Cooper, and as you pass me I would like you to tell me the name of the person behind you."

He assumed all the kids knew each other's name already, and if not, it was a good exercise for them to get to know one another.

"Tommy, I want you to lead the way."

"All right!" He tossed his hand in the air and hurried to the front. "Come on guys and lady," he emphasized. "Kayla, you can stand behind me."

Not only was this kid a natural born leader he was a ladies' man. Cooper didn't want to pick favorites, but this kid was making it hard not to.

A single file line formed, and as Tommy led the way, Cooper learned the names of each of his campers, making sure everyone stayed on track to the clearing. The last thing he needed was to lose a kid on the first day.

Once everyone found a cut piece of wood to sit on, he walked to the middle of the circle. All eyes were on him, and he thought about the summer when he was one of the kids, staring up at Bob and waiting to hear about all of the cool things he had planned for the summer. Cooper remembered being so excited for what was to come, and he hoped he would be able to put that same kind of enthusiasm into these kids.

"Now that I know everyone's name we can get started."

"Are we going to look for moose?" Kyle asked.

"I don't think so," Cooper said, and Kyle looked up at him with annoyance on his face.

"That's lame." Kyle crossed his arms over his chest and slouched forward in disappointment.

This was not going the way he wanted it to. He should've known he'd have a wiseass in his group. It was the first day, though, and he didn't want to send the little punk home disappointed.

"Tell you what, Kyle. If you behave for the rest of the summer, meaning I never have to take you aside and have a conversation, then on our last day I will take you to look for moose."

"You're not pulling my chain, are you?"

"I wouldn't do that," Cooper said. "The first thing about the wilderness is always be honest with the people you are with. If you want to have any chance at survival, you need to be able to trust each other. Got it?"

He received a collective nod from all the kids and felt relief as he continued on, explaining what he had in store for them for the rest of the summer.

"You'll learn about animal tracks, how to identify the animal, how long it's been since they'd been by, and if they're travelling alone. That way you can prevent yourself from coming face to face with something you might not want."

"Like a lion!" Tommy said.

"There are no lions in New Hampshire, stupid."

"Hey," Cooper said, pointing his finger and feeling very much like an adult. "There will be no name calling. That's strike one. Two more and no moose expedition."

"Fine," Kyle grumbled, slouching forward again.

"While there aren't lions in these woods, there are bobcats. Lucky for us, they're usually more scared of us than we are of them. They are nocturnal. Does anyone know what that means?"

"They only come out at night like bats!" Kayla called out.

"Exactly. But in the winter, they are known to come out during the day in order to hunt for prey."

"Have you ever seen one before?" Robbie, a dark-skinned boy with black hair said.

"I have."

"Liar!" Kyle called out, and Cooper was tempted to give him another strike, but he had a feeling the kid needed a little leniency.

"There was a den up by my parents' farm when I was a kid. We left them alone and eventually they moved on. I've also seen a lion in the wild," he said, knowing if he was a kid he'd be fascinated by the idea.

"Yeah right," Kyle said, and at this point Cooper just chuckled at his lack of belief.

"Where?" Rico asked his eyes wide with curiosity.

"Africa. Tanzania to be exact."

"No way!" Tommy and a few of the other boys said.

"What else did you see?"

"Giraffes, hippos, gorillas, zebra, elephants, and a rhino."

All eyes stared up at him like he was the most interesting thing on the planet; even Kyle's mouth was ajar as he listened. Apparently, Cooper had converted the skeptic.

He spent the next ten minutes answering questions about all the animals he had seen. At one point, he felt like he was being interrogated with the way the questions flew out of these kids. As soon as he answered one, three more were flung his way. But it was as if he was made for this—sharing his adventures with these kids who genuinely cared. Maybe he would plant a seed in their heads and some of them would become world travelers themselves.

He looked down at his watch, amazed at how quickly their time had passed. Earlier in the day he had no idea how he would keep ten kids occupied for six hours, and here he was not ready to say goodbye yet.

Tommy, his little leader of the pack, led the kids back to the main area where they could meet their parents. Cooper followed closely behind, making sure each kid arrived safely.

"I'll see you guys tomorrow. Remember sunscreen, bug spray, and what else?"

"Sneakers," they said in unison.

He had been surprised to see some of the kids wearing flip-flops. For what he had planned that wasn't going to work. Safety was the number one factor when it came to working with these kids. He was responsible for them, and he wasn't going to let them get hurt because they weren't wearing the proper footwear.

He gave each kid a high five as they made their way to where their parents were waiting to pick them up near the parking lot.

One of the other counselors, Shelley—who couldn't have been a day over eighteen—approached him. "Hi Cooper. How was your first day?" she asked a slight blush spreading across her cheeks.

"Went really well. How about you? Handling that group of girls okay?" Shelley was with a group of girls that ranged between the ages of eleven and twelve. If given the choice between gauging his eyeballs out with dull pencils or taking that group, Cooper would definitely choose the pencils.

"Oh you know it's easy for me. I remember being that young," she said as if she was twenty years their senior instead of six which made Cooper laugh. Cooper could tell when a girl was trying to flirt with him, and he needed to put an end to this before she got any ideas in her head.

"It wasn't that long ago. I remember when you were a little girl in pigtails coming to the Fall Festival and fighting with your mom over not wanting to leave the bounce house."

A flash of embarrassment streaked across her face, and while Cooper felt a little bad, he knew it couldn't have been helped. It was better to nip it in the bud.

"That was like forever ago," she said with a wave of her hands. "Oh, my ride's here. I'll talk to you later." Shelley ran off, and Cooper sighed in relief.

"Cooper! Cooper!" He heard Tommy calling his name just before the little guy grabbed his hand. "Come meet my mom."

"Okay buddy, lead the way since you're so good at it." He followed Tommy, and when they broke through the now dwindling crowd of campers and parents, his heart slammed against his chest.

"Mom! This is my counselor, Cooper. Cooper this is

my mom. She worries a lot so she wanted to meet you."

"You?" Sarah exclaimed. Her shocked tone a reflection of exactly how he felt.

Tommy turned back to Sarah, tugging on her blouse and causing the V neck to dip even lower, reminding him of what was beneath the white fabric. "Mom, Cooper went to Africa and he saw elephants and lions and giraffes. Can we go to Africa?"

"Tommy, get in the car," Sarah said, her voice calm and cool even though he could still see the shock in her dark brown eyes.

"But Mom!"

Sarah kneeled down to Tommy's level. "I can't wait to hear all about your day, but I want to talk to Cooper for a minute. Is that okay?"

"I guess so."

"I'll be right there. Promise."

Sarah waited for Tommy to get in the car before she turned back to him.

"You're Tommy's mom?" Cooper asked, knowing the information as it was just displayed right in front of him, but he couldn't seem to wrap his head around it. Of all the kids, all the camps, her son just happened to be in his group for the next two weeks. What the hell were the chances?

"Yes, and I want to make sure that he never finds out anything about us."

Frustration boiled beneath the surface, and Cooper stepped closer to her, lowering his voice so not to draw attention. "What do you think? That I'm going to brag about it to a seven-year-old? Give me some credit for crying out loud."

"You're right. I'm sorry. I just don't know how to

navigate this. You and Tommy were supposed to be two completely separate parts of my life and somehow this happened." An annoyed laugh slipped from her pretty lips. "I swear someone up there must hate me."

"Or maybe someone up there is trying to tell you something."

"And what exactly would that be?"

"That you shouldn't try to keep your life in parts. Maybe someone is trying to tell you that there's no reason why you can't have all of it."

He had been terrified at the thought of her having a kid, but now that he knew Tommy was her kid it didn't bother him like the thought once did. Tommy was a cool fucking kid with a good head on his shoulders. He wouldn't mind spending time with him, especially if it meant he could spend time with Sarah.

She ran a hand through her hair. "I'm not doing this right now."

"Doing what? Listening to the voice of reason?"

"Is that what you think you are?"

"Someone has to be. You're so stuck in your head, lost in this stupid notion where you can't have a social life when really the only person you're hurting is yourself."

"I said I'm not doing this."

"Fine. Walk away. I'm getting pretty used to seeing your back anyway."

"Me?" she snapped, causing a few people to look their way. She stepped closer to him, and he had to swallow down the desire to snake his hand around her waist and yank her up against him. "You're the one that keeps leaving. At Matt and Shay's you walked away first. At Ellie's store, you again."

"So, you're paying attention?"

"What is that even supposed to mean?"

"It just seems that you're so consumed in your own life that it's a surprise you see anyone else but yourself."

"That's where you're going with this? Really? That's real mature, Cooper."

"What can I say? The truth hurts sometimes."

Her lip twitched with annoyance and it was the sexiest damn thing. He wanted to take that lip between his teeth and nibble on the plump flesh while he ran his hands over her body.

She held up both of her hands, taking a deep breath. "This isn't going to work."

"What isn't going to work?"

"This." She waved her finger between them and then turned her attention to Tommy who was staring down at a tablet. "You being his counselor. I don't want to but I think I have to pull him from your group."

"Don't be ridiculous."

"I don't know how else we can make this work."

"Easy. You drop him off just like you did this morning and you pick him up just like you're doing now. We never have to see each other if that's what you want."

She was quiet for a second, and Cooper wondered what the hell was going through her mind. She was a hard person to crack, and he never knew what she was thinking. Even if he could get a peek on the inside, he had a feeling it would be a complicated web that he wouldn't be able to decipher anyway.

"I don't want that," she said so softly he almost didn't hear her.

"You don't?"

She looked up at him, her dark brown eyes catching his

and slaying him into a thousand pathetic little pieces. "Of course I don't. But it's not about what I want. I have to do what is right for my son, and I'm sorry if you don't understand that, but that's just how it has to be."

"I get it."

"Wait what? You do?"

"Tommy's a great kid. Really special. Most kids don't just turn out that way on their own. Whatever you're doing, you're doing it right."

He hoped his words would take back the previous ones he had said a couple of months ago.

A smile touched the edge of her mouth, and he wanted to kiss it so he could watch it spread further. But then he saw the tears in her eyes, and all he wanted to do was pull her against him and comfort her.

"You have no idea how much that means to me."

He reached forward, tucking her hair behind her ear because he couldn't stand being that close to her for another second without touching her. "I think I do."

When she blinked up the tears were gone, but her eyes still shimmered. "I should go."

"Only if you promise you won't punish Tommy because of us."

"He'll see you tomorrow morning," she said and stepped back, making him feel the loss of her closeness almost instantly.

He didn't want to let her go, but she wasn't his. Not yet at least. She would be, though. He was sure of it now.

She rounded the car, and he called out to her. She stopped, looking back at him.

"Congratulations by the way."

"For what?"

"On your new found fame. I knew you could do it. I had no doubts."

She pulled the sunglasses off her head and slipped them over her eyes. "Don't worry, I won't forget the little people," she said and just like that, the Sarah that she kept hidden so deep inside came out to play.

Chapter 11

She wasn't sick. Nope. Absolutely not. She did not have time to be sick. Not when she had a flood of new orders sitting in her inbox and another hundred emails she hadn't even opened yet. Her to-do list needed its own to-do list. This was the worst possible time to not be a hundred percent.

And it was the summer. Who got sick in the summer? Definitely not her. But she couldn't ignore the boulder that decided to implant itself in her nasal cavity. She had to have swallowed rocks because why else would her throat hurt so damn bad?

It was okay. This was nothing some vitamins, a little cough medicine and a nasal decongestant couldn't fix. Luckily, she still had some in the house from when Tommy got sick this past winter. She was a mom damn it, and she could handle a small case of the sniffles.

She went to the kitchen made herself a cup of hot green tea and downed the recommended doses. Once the meds kicked in she would be as good as new.

Her cell phone rang, and she looked at the screen, immediately answering it when she saw Bex's name pop up.

"Hey Sarah. You busy?"

"No, not at all."

"You okay? You don't sound right."

"Just a little cold. No big deal. What can I do for you today?"

"I'm doing the cover for Vogue."

"Oh my god, that's amazing. Congratulations!"

"Thank you. Now this is the best part. Are you sitting? Because you should be sitting."

Sarah sat down in one of the chairs at the kitchen table, the movement using way too much energy and causing her to slump forward. "I'm sitting," she said.

"Perfect. Because this is going to knock you on your ass. They loved the necklace you made me, the one to go with the coral dress so much that they want me to wear it on the cover."

"My necklace? On the cover of Vogue?"

"Isn't that fantastic?"

Sarah didn't know what to say. That magazine was an iconic symbol of fashion. She grew up flipping through the pages, admiring the models, the clothes, the jewelry, and hairstyles. Never in a million years would she ever have imagined that one of her own pieces would one day grace the pages, no less the cover.

She was speechless. There were no words to even begin to describe the emotions running through her.

"Sarah, you there?"

"Yeah," she managed, her voice shaking.

"I don't know if you heard me. Your necklace is going to be on the cover of Vogue."

No matter how many times Bex said it, it just didn't seem to sink in. It was a dream come true.

"I heard you," Sarah finally said. "I'm just…"

"Speechless? I figured as much. Take some time to process."

"Okay."

"Listen, they need me back on set, but I'd love to discuss a few other things with you. Can I call you later?"

"Absolutely!"

"Awesome. Talk then. Bye." Bex hung up, and Sarah lowered her hand to the table, letting the phone fall from her grasp.

Excitement bubbled inside of her until tears filled her eyes. Damn sickness was breaking her down and making her a weepy mess. She tried to fight the overwhelming emotion, but she was a prisoner to its strength.

Tears filled her eyes as she let out an excited laugh. She jumped up from the table with renewed vigor only to realize how bad of an idea that was. She managed to grab hold of the chair before her weak legs gave out on her, and she eased herself back down.

Maybe if she just closed her eyes for a few minutes, she would feel better. She'd celebrate by going down to Sweet Dream Bakery and treating herself to a midweek cupcake. Yes, that's exactly what she was going to do... after she closed her eyes for a few minutes.

She rested her head against the cool wood of the table and relaxed.

When she finally opened her eyes, she knew without even looking at a clock that her eyes were closed for a lot longer than she'd hoped. Her neck was killing her from being at such an awkward angle.

She dragged her hand across the table, searching for her phone. It took a few passes before she finally found it. Expecting to have only slept for an hour tops she was stunned to see she had slept the entire morning away and most of the afternoon.

Somehow it was already two-thirty, and she needed to go pick Tommy up from camp. She tried to stand, but her legs felt like they weighed nine hundred pounds... her head not too far behind.

The medicine she took had done absolutely nothing as the boulder in her nasal cavity only seemed to have grown.

While all she wanted to do was crawl to her bed and collapse on the nice warm comforter, she couldn't. Moms didn't get days off. They couldn't call in sick. She needed to pick Tommy up from camp, and once he was home and had dinner she could start on her to-do list. It would just be another late night, that was all.

She managed to push herself up and grab her keys and purse. The walk to the car felt like she was walking to the ends of the earth. When she finally got there, she used the little energy she had left to pull the door open and slide into the driver's seat.

The chills that had been wracking her body dissolved to the hot waves of lava moving through her veins.

She ignored the sudden wave of nausea, the raging inferno creeping up her neck and the banging in her head and pulled out of the driveway.

***

Cooper waited with Tommy for Sarah to arrive while Tommy talked with the other kids. Sarah was not one to be late. If anything, she was the type of person who would show up a half hour early.

He was starting to worry and about to call her when he spotted her car pulling into the parking lot. She came to a slow stop a few feet away.

Cooper was sick of avoiding her. Sick of giving her space. Hadn't it been long enough? If Cooper was going to get anywhere with her he needed to be accessible. This space bullshit wasn't working, and he was over it.

As he approached the car he was surprised to see Sarah resting her head on the steering wheel.

He tapped gently on the window, and she lifted her head like it weighed way more than it should. She hit the button, and he waited for the window to lower.

"Hi," she said, her voice scratchy and harsh.

"Are you okay?" he asked, noticing her pale skin with a fresh gleam of perspiration. Her usual beautiful dark brown eyes were sunken and glossy.

She inhaled a deep breath that caused her to cough uncontrollably for a few moments. When she finally stopped, she looked at him obviously trying to be as convincing as possible that she was okay, but failing terribly. "I will be."

"You don't look too good."

"Thanks," she said with her usual aloofness, but it was weak, exposing a hint of her vulnerability.

He lifted his aviators and winked. "Any time."

Tommy waved goodbye to the group of kids and ran for the car, arms flailing like the excited seven-year-old he was. He hopped in the car, slamming the door with a loud bang. Sarah winced, reaching for her head and rubbing circles at her temple.

"Hey, sweetie. How was your day?" she asked, and Cooper admired her dedication to her son. Despite how horrible she looked—and must have felt—she still showed him kindness and affection.

"It was great! Cooper taught us about animal tracks and how to know how long it's been since an animal has been there so when you're in the woods alone you know if it's safe or not. Did you know Cooper went to Africa and saw lions and elephants and zebras?" She glanced at Cooper for a second, and he shrugged. Tommy continued, but Cooper could see the struggle in Sarah to focus on what he was saying.

"We should go," she finally said. It was as if she was in slow motion as she reached for the shifter. He couldn't let her drive away. Not like this. If something happened to her or Tommy he'd never forgive himself.

He opened the door, and Sarah turned to him, surprise in her dark eyes. "What are you doing?"

"You're not driving," he stated.

"Don't be ridiculous."

"I'm not. You are. Tommy get your seat belt on. I'm driving you guys home. Your mom's not feeling too good."

Sarah stared at him with her eyebrows furrowed. "How are you going to get back?"

"I have four siblings in this town, several others by marriage, as well as my parents and grandparents. I think I'll be able to find a ride."

"Let me at least wipe the steering wheel down." She leaned across the console and grabbed for a box of antiseptic wipes, making him laugh. Even sick she still felt the need to make sure everyone else was protected from germs. With a high immune system and the fact that he rarely got sick, he wrapped his arms around her and hoisted her out of the car.

"Cooper!" she cried out. "Are you crazy?"

"Depends who you ask."

She rolled her eyes. "You're impossible."

"Lucky for me, you're too sick to fight back."

She mumbled a response then rested her head against his chest, letting him carry her to the passenger seat without a single objection. He liked having her in his arms, feeling the curves of her body melding against his.

This woman was the opposite of everything he ever looked for. She was rational and structured. Reserved and proud. But beneath her control he could see a woman who needed to be set free from the restraints she put on herself. A woman who, if he wasn't careful, he could fall in love with.

And that realization was by far scarier than any flesh hungry animal he'd ever encountered.

Chapter 12

Sarah didn't remember the car ride home. As soon as Cooper put her in the passenger seat she completely passed out. She didn't remember getting home or going to bed, and she definitely didn't remember changing into pajamas.

She looked around her bedroom, completely confused. Light still sprinkled in from outside, so it couldn't have been too late. Unless it was the next day.

Then that would mean she'd have missed Bex's call. And what about Tommy? She had to make him dinner and prepare his lunch for tomorrow. She also meant to do laundry because he was on his last pair of clean shorts. She pushed up, but her arms were like Jell-O, and she couldn't manage to hold her weight, collapsing against the bed in a pathetic state.

Sweat lined her brow, the temperature in the room rising by a hundred degrees. She tried so hard to fight because, sick or not, she had to show up, but she just couldn't.

Everything in her body hurt. Muscles she didn't even know that she had ached. The thought of standing made her stomach twist in protesting knots.

Her eyes blurred as the pain in her head throbbed with unrelenting pulses. She managed to kick the comforter off of her and curl up into a ball. She just needed five more minutes. Then she would try again.

She let her heavy eyes fall shut until the sprinkling of light slipped away, consuming her in darkness.

A touch of cold on her forehead woke her and felt like she managed to escape the fiery depths of hell and float toward heaven. She relished in the coolness that spread through her face and down her neck. She tried to open her eyes, but she didn't have the energy to manage. Instead she pressed further into the soft cool touch that caressed her and fell back to sleep.

She dreamed of Cooper, stroking her back and assuring her she'd be okay in no time. She wanted to tell him she was fine, that she didn't get sick, but every time she tried to speak it felt like razor blades slicing across her throat. So instead of arguing with him, she nestled in closer to his soothing strokes, letting this beautiful figment of her imagination take care of her.

Dreams turned to a world of blackness, and even though she wanted to relish in his touch, she couldn't fight the dark cloud that pushed her into slumber.

Her shirt was soaked through when she awoke again, her forehead a dripping mess. She could feel her hair matted to her cheeks. Feel the heat exit her body, leaving her in a cold sweat that turned to uncontrollable chills that wracked her body mercilessly.

The desire to climb back under the covers and seek warmth was so strong, but the sheets were wet and cold, making her retreat to the other side of the bed in search of a clean, dry place. She found it and collapsed into the mattress just as a warm gentle hand came down on her back, rubbing calming strokes.

The comfort of the mattress disappeared, and she was being carried away. She had no idea where she was going, but it didn't matter, because whatever was holding her was warm and strong.

"Tommy, where does your mom keep the sheets?" she thought she heard, but it was so far away and muffled.

She tried to hold up her hand to point toward the linen closet but only made it a couple inches before her hand fell back against her chest.

The warmth disappeared, and she wanted to cry out and pull it back, but before she could she fell back asleep.

The next time she awoke, she was no longer wet, but the cold seeped into her veins, turning her to a shivering block of ice.

"So cold."

The bed sunk beside her and arms pulled her tight against that comforting warmth from earlier that she had missed. "Better, baby?"

"Cooper?" she managed.

"Right here. What do you need?"

"You."

"I'm not going anywhere."

"Even in my dreams you're perfect."

She heard his sexy laugh, and she wanted to tell him it was her dream and he didn't get to make fun of her, but he shushed her with a sweet caress against her cheek and sleep consumed her again.

***

Cooper held Sarah in his arms. Her hands were ice cold so he pulled the blankets more firmly around them. He didn't know what else to do. The only person he knew that had tons of experience at any of this was his own mom who he had called six times since he'd gotten Sarah home.

She told him to keep Sarah hydrated, which was impossible for someone who was basically unconscious. Then she had told him just to let her sleep it off, but when he checked on her and she was burning with fever, her body dripping with sweat, he couldn't just leave her like that.

Luckily, Tommy was a huge help, knowing exactly where everything was and leading the way like the natural born leader he was. But Cooper was afraid of the poor kid catching whatever plague Sarah had, so after a few phone calls he managed to get in touch with Tommy's best friend's mother, Gina, who offered to take him.

Now it was just him and Sarah in her house. He wondered if she would be mad once she came to and realized that he took control of the situation since she was such a control freak. Even when he'd asked Tommy where the sheets were, he felt her arm move to try and point him in a direction, but she'd been too weak. Stubborn even when her body was making it impossible for her to function.

He looked down at her flushed cheeks and the bags beneath her eyes, yet she was still the most beautiful woman he'd ever seen. If only she could believe in him enough to know just how badly he wanted to be a part of her life.

He could still travel and post pictures to his accounts, write about experiences, and keep his fans happy, but in between, instead of seeking out a new location, he could come home for long stretches of time and be with her. Be the man she needed.

In a perfect world, it was the perfect solution. But their world wasn't perfect. It was much more complicated than that. Sarah needed a man who wasn't going to leave for long lengths of time, and that wasn't something he could promise her. She needed someone who would always be there for her and Tommy, who would put them above himself at all times.

Cooper didn't think he was selfish, but he wasn't about to pull the plug on a career that had taken him years to build.

And maybe that did make him a little selfish, but he'd earned that right, hadn't he?

His fans, while loyal, were starting to get restless, dying to know where he was going to be off to next. It had been almost a year since he came home, and he had been posting never before seen pictures from his archives but they wanted more. They lived vicariously through him and wanted the adventure to continue. That couldn't happen if he stayed in Red Maple Falls.

He needed to go somewhere exotic that elicited that strong feeling of wanderlust, making people cling to his every photo and description as if they were experiencing it themselves. He owed that to them because without them, he was no one. They gave him the chance to follow his dreams and design a career around his passion. How could he walk away from them?

Sarah stirred in his arms, and he loosened his hold on her to give her the freedom to move as she needed. Her hand curled into his shirt, and she pulled herself closer to him, molding her body to his. He swallowed down the desire having her curves pressed flush against him did to his insides and rested his hand back on her lower back.

"You're so warm," she mumbled in her sleep, and he smiled at the adorableness of it.

"Go back to sleep," he said, brushing her hair off of her face. "You need your rest."

"What if you're gone when I wake up?"

"I already told you that I'm not going anywhere."

"But you will leave eventually."

He realized she wasn't talking about just now or in the next few weeks. She was talking about the future. She had the same thoughts even in her sick rattled mind that he himself was wrestling with.

He rubbed small circles with his thumb against her arm. "Yeah," he said, his voice heavy with unease.

"That's why I can't fall in love with you."

Even though she probably had no idea what the hell she was saying, hearing those words fall from her pretty lips were a direct hit to his heart.

It made sense—why she pushed him away and continued to push him away even when he'd tried to apologize. How she got mad every time they bumped into each other because she was probably trying so hard to avoid him.

But all her attempts at keeping him at arms-length failed because the distance made him see what he would have been too blind to have noticed if it was right in front of him. For the first time in his life, he was falling, and he was falling hard.

He smiled down at her, her eyes shut, long lashes brushing against her skin, fingers still curled around the fabric of his shirt and let the realization sink in. "I think I already have."

Chapter 13

The next morning, Sarah woke still feeling like she was hit by a bus but able to open her eyes and pull herself up to lean against the headboard. She looked down, confused at the thin black tank top and matching pajama shorts.

Everything from the moment she pulled into the parking lot to pick up Tommy was a blur. She pressed a hand to her forehead, trying to remember the last twenty-four hours. Bits in pieces flashed into her mind, but she couldn't decipher what was real and what was a dream.

It would have to wait; she needed to check on Tommy. The boy was self-sufficient, she had made sure of that, but he had been practically unsupervised all day and all night. She wouldn't be surprised if she found him watching TV in his underwear surrounded by empty containers of junk food.

She went to stand, but she had given herself too much credit. As soon as she got up, the room tilted on its axis, and she stumbled back onto the bed. The boulder that had implanted itself in her sinus cavity was still there and obviously throwing off her equilibrium.

With a deep breath, she stood again, determined to get to the living room. She moved, ignoring the uncomfortable fog in her brain, and reached out for the footboard.

"Look who decided to join the living again." Cooper's voice floated into the room, and Sarah froze.

He was here? *Oh shit.* Did that mean everything she thought was a dream actually wasn't?

She went to answer him when her legs wobbled

beneath her. Before she could move or say anything, she was in Cooper's arms. He carried her back bed and eased her down against the mattress.

"You need to take it easy."

"No, I need to check on Tommy and make him breakfast. And I need to get back to work. I'm so behind now. Oh my god, Bex Shepard was supposed to call me back yesterday. Did I miss her call?"

She went to sit up to search for her phone when Cooper's hand came down on her shoulder and held her in place.

"I'm taking care of everything. You just need to get better."

"What do you mean you're taking care of everything? Where is my son?"

"I didn't want him to get sick too so I sent him to Gina's. I hope that's okay."

The panic that began to build faded. "Yeah, of course. I would have done the same thing if I could have." She pushed her hair off her face. "What about you? Aren't you scared of getting sick?"

He shrugged. "I wasn't leaving you alone."

"I would've been fine."

He laughed loud, his tone mocking. "Can you ever just admit that you need help?"

"I didn't."

"Baby, you couldn't even hold yourself up. Besides, how do you think you got into those clothes?"

She looked down at the black tank and matching shorts again. "You put these on me?"

"I changed you twice. The first time into something comfortable and the second time because you sweated right through the others. And don't look at me like that. If you've forgotten, I've seen every inch of your naked body up close and personal."

She swallowed at his words, forgetting how bad her throat hurt and causing a disgusting coughing fit.

Cooper turned to her nightstand, grabbed a bottle of water, and handed it to her. "Drink this." She took the bottle from his hand and took a big sip, letting the cool liquid soothe the rawness in her throat. "I'll pick up some cough drops when I go to the store later."

She shook her head. "No, you've done enough. You should go."

He ran a frustrated hand through his hair, causing the veins in his arms to bulge. "You were such a better patient when you were unconscious."

"I wasn't unconscious. I was just sleeping."

"Either way, you were much easier to deal with when you couldn't argue with me."

"I'm not arguing."

"No? Because it sounds an awful lot like it if you ask me."

"Well, I'm not." Even she knew she was being a bitch, but having Cooper in her house, taking care of her, was too much. She wanted to hate him because it would be easier when he left because they both knew it was only a matter of time before he did.

He being in her home made her want things that would only hurt her in the long run. She was only trying to protect her heart, was that so wrong? But how could she just discount everything he had done for her in the past twenty-four hours? She really just wanted to wrap her arms around him and thank him for not only taking care of her, but for taking care of Tommy, too.

"I'm sorry," she finally said, letting her tone carry more emotion than she normally would allow. "You don't deserve my attitude after all that you've done for me."

"It's okay," he said, sitting down beside her on the bed. He rested his hand against her cheek, and she pressed into it, loving the warmth of it on her skin.

"I get it," he said, and she looked up into the blue depths of his eyes, searching for more of an explanation. She didn't have to search long or hard before he articulated it. "I'm going to leave eventually. I have to. It's my job. And I know that scares you, but it scares me, too, because now that I know you, I can't imagine my life without you."

"This is crazy. We barely even know each other."

"I know that you're fiercely independent. Strong willed and driven. That you love your son more than anything on this earth and that you live and breathe for him. I know that you're an amazing mom, an insanely talented business woman and designer, that you don't let life knock you down without a fight. You're stubborn and persistent. You can be cold and hide behind a façade, but that's only because you sometimes get scared and it's easier to pretend that you don't have any weaknesses than admit to the fear. And I know that you're scared to open your heart to whatever this is between us. But sometimes no matter how hard you try to control something you have to accept that you're just the passenger and you have no control over what happens next. We can try to stay away from each other, put an end to this, but even if we do, I have a feeling life will keep throwing us in each other's path. So this is my long-winded way of telling you that I don't care how much you push me away. How many times you tell me to go away. I'm not leaving. Not yet at least. So let me take care of you. We'll figure out the rest when that time comes."

After a speech like that how could she say no? It didn't matter how long they knew each other—a day, a week, or a year, he knew her better than anyone. He had seen all sides of her, and he hadn't walked away yet. Why not take each day at a time and, like he said, figure it out when the time came?

"Okay," she said, and she laughed when his baby blue eyes widened in surprise which only sent her into another coughing fit.

He nudged the bottle of water in her hand, and she took another generous sip.

"You're really not going to argue with me?"

"No."

"Really? Because I was prepared. I can go for at least an hour more."

She smiled and tugged on his shirt, pulling him closer so she could rest her head against his chest. "Save it. I'm sure you'll need it in the future. For now, I just want to be here."

***

When Sarah fell asleep, Cooper slipped away and headed to the store to stock up on supplies and extra bags of cough drops. He also made a call to Dr. Stevens and got her an appointment for the next morning. The doctor assumed it was the summer flu which there wasn't much he could do for, but Cooper didn't like the sound of Sarah's cough and made the appointment for her anyway.

He would bet money she'd have something to say about him making her an appointment, but he was ready for that fight. She was an independent and strong woman, and he wasn't going to let her scare him away because she didn't know how to let others help her. He was determined to show her it was okay to not always be in control. It would be a long process he was sure of but he was also sure that he was up for the challenge.

His cell phone buzzed in his pocket, and he slipped it out to see who was texting him. He was surprised to see his buddy Gray's name flash on the screen with a new text. Gray was another travel blogger he had met in Brazil at Lencois Maranhenses National Park while taking in the natural phenomenon of the turquoise lagoons surrounded by beautiful white sand dunes. They had got to talking and wound up travelling together for a few months before going their separate ways.

They had kept in touch over the years, meeting up occasionally when they happened to be in the same place at the same time. Not only did they share a passion for travel but both dreamed of walking the entire length of the Great Wall.

And they were going to do it. They had it planned, emailing each other for months until they'd finally set a date to make it happen. But Gray broke his leg skiing in the Swiss Alps and they had to cancel.

If he was texting now, it only meant one thing: he was ready. Cooper opened the text, knowing what it was going to say before even reading it.

Hey, my man. The Great Wall. This September. You in?

He knew it. Gray said once he was a hundred percent there'd be no stopping him. He was going to do it whether Cooper was in or not.

After doing the math, they figured they could do it in roughly eighteen months, give or take depending on weather. It was a long commitment, and a few months ago Cooper would have jumped at the opportunity. After all, it was an epic adventure—the ultimate check on his bucket list. But now... Eighteen months away from Sarah seemed like a damn lifetime. Would she even wait for him to get back?

He sure as hell wouldn't expect her to. But how did he turn down the chance to do the one thing that he always wanted to do so badly?

Even after Gray got hurt, Cooper thought about doing it alone once he'd finished backpacking through Europe with a group of people who religiously followed his blog. But then Matt got engaged and Cooper decided to cut short his trip and come home. He hadn't looked back since. At least not until now.

He needed to give Gray an answer, but he had no idea what that answer was. He stared at his phone as his mind and heart tugged relentlessly back and forth, both parts of each taking different sides and making it impossible for Cooper to make a decision.

Not sure yet. When do you need an answer by?

He sent the text and waited.

Don't skip out on me now! Leaving second week in September with or without you.

A part of Cooper wanted to say fuck it and just say yes. Why the hell not? But the other part of him refused to let that happen. He typed a quick response.

I'll let you know.

Then he shoved his phone back in his pocket before he could regret it.

Chapter 14

It had been a week since Sarah had the plague from hell, but she was starting a second round of antibiotics thanks to the upper respiratory infection that was still lingering. She was finally feeling better, though, and was looking forward to catching up on work.

Cooper had taken care of not only her and Tommy, but also fielding her calls and responding to emails when she didn't have the energy to lift her arms.

She had been panicking over her missed call with Bex Shepard, but apparently Cooper took the call, explained the situation, and in the process completely charmed Bex's socks off. Bex had sent a beautiful flower arrangement with a get well soon card and a side note to say Cooper was a keeper.

Even over the phone the man was impossible to resist. She shook her head at the thought, smiling with amusement. He was impossible all right. Making a doctor appointment for her without even consenting her, even if she did need to go and probably wouldn't have until it was really bad, bringing her and Tommy takeout from the Happy Apple so she didn't have to worry about cooking, picking Tommy up in the morning on his way to camp and bringing him home after.

Impossible, but unbelievably sweet. Each second he spent in her home, he became more and more a part of it. A part of her. She couldn't imagine going into the kitchen when she was finished working for the day and not seeing him there, unpacking dinner and telling Tommy to go wash up. She couldn't imagine not kissing him goodnight outside by his truck, beneath the stars because she still hadn't budged on him sleeping over.

Though, he was breaking down her resolve a little bit more every day. She was scared for Tommy to get too attached. She could manage the broken heart if Cooper decided to leave one day, but she couldn't handle seeing her son's heart break and knowing it was her fault for not being more careful about who she'd let into his life.

For now, what they had worked. To Tommy, Cooper was his camp counselor who stopped by to hang out for a while every day. She could deal with that. By not letting him stay the night, she was creating a much needed distance to keep Cooper and Tommy's bond from becoming too strong that it would hurt Tommy.

Maybe she was being a fool for trying to keep her son from having a male figure in his life or maybe for allowing it knowing that Cooper's time with them had an unexpected expiration date. She wasn't sure what was right and what was wrong. All she knew was that she couldn't push Cooper out of her life. Not again. She wanted to spend as much time with him as she could and take advantage of the now without worrying too much about the future.

Right this second, though, she needed to focus on work. She sat down at her desk with a cup of coffee and wrote a to-do list so she would know exactly what needed to be done and what needed to be tackled first.

Each check off the list was like a weight lifted from her shoulders. By the time she had all but a couple things left to do, she heard the front door open and close and Tommy's voice carrying down the hallway. "Mom!"

She put the necklace she was working on down and

went out to meet him in the kitchen. The first thing she noticed was Cooper casually leaning against the counter, looking effortlessly beautiful, and then her eyes landed on Tommy and the sleeping bag he had his arms wrapped around.

"What's this?" she asked, nodding toward the sleeping bag.

"Me and Coop are going camping!" he exclaimed, his smile going wide and highlighting the adorable freckles on his cheeks.

"Excuse me?" Sarah asked, knowing that she did not okay this.

Cooper pushed off the counter and walked toward her with purpose, but stopped just shy of acting on the desire in his gaze. "How was your day? You're looking much better," he said, giving her that charming smirk, probably hoping to distract her or sugar her up. She wasn't falling for his trickery.

"Don't change the subject. Camping, Cooper? Were you planning on asking me?"

Cooper's lip quirked as if he found her annoyance funny which only annoyed her more. "I believe my exact words, Tommy," Cooper said, rustling Tommy's hair, "is that if it was okay with your mother we could set up camp in the backyard tonight."

Tommy kicked at the ground, clearly aware that he was in the wrong. "Mom, can we? Please? I promise to be good and eat my vegetables for the rest of the summer. And I promise to clean up my messes. Please, Mom. Please?"

"We don't even have a tent. Unless you plan on roughing it in sleeping bags. And if that's the case, absolutely not. You'll both be eaten alive by mosquitoes."

"I have a tent," Cooper said.

"Of course you do."

He shrugged. "That tent was my home many times. It's a good one. Keeps out the bugs and whatever else is lurking out there in the fenced in backyard. And you are more than welcome to join us."

"Yeah, Mom. Come on! It'll be fun. We can roast marshmallows and make s'mores. And tell scary stories."

"Yeah, come on, Sarah," Cooper said, and Sarah cut him a look.

"You want to hype him up on sugar and then scare him with stories? Sounds like a bad combination if you ask me."

"Can you stop overthinking things for once and just say yes. It'll be fun." Cooper leaned in, his breath grazing the sensitive skin by her ear. "We both know how much you love fun," he said as he pulled back, leaving her in his delicious scent, heat running through her veins and right to her core.

She swallowed, forcing the sensations and emotions down. There was a time and a place and in front of Tommy was definitely not either.

"Please, Mom!" Tommy pressed his hands together then dropped to his knees in a desperate plea.

"Okay," she said and laughed when Tommy threw his arms in the air. He jumped up, giving Cooper a high five.

"I'll go get everything together," he said, running from the kitchen.

Once he was out of sight, Sarah turned to Cooper. "Is this your way of getting around the no sleepover rule?"

His hand snaked around her waist, hauling her tight against him. "Maybe."

She could feel the bulge in his pants against her center,

and if Tommy wasn't in the other room she would have dropped to her knees and showed Cooper just how much she loved a little fun. Instead she placed her hand on his chest and looked up into his eyes.

"What's the matter?" he asked, tucking her hair behind her ear. "I promise to stay on my side of the tent."

She laughed. "It's not that."

"Then what is it?"

"Tommy's getting attached to you, and I'm worried."

"Don't be."

"How can I not be? For the past seven years, I have done everything in my power to protect him. If he gets too attached and you leave, what kind of mother does that make me for not protecting him from the disappointment?"

The look in Cooper's eyes said things she couldn't quite read; it worried her.

"Hey," he finally said, tilting her chin up so he was looking directly into her eyes. "I'll never disappoint him. Even if I have to go I won't just leave him behind… or you. I probably should have told you sooner, but I'm not easy to get rid of."

"Do you plan on leaving soon?" she asked, hating how fearful she sounded.

He ran a hand over his face like he needed a second to think then let out a slow breath. Before he could say anything, Tommy came barreling in the kitchen with his pillows and two bags filled with toys.

"Where do you think you're going with all that?" Sarah asked, her hand landing on her hip as she turned to him.

"Outside," he said a look of pure confusion on his face. "We're camping, aren't we?"

"I got this," Cooper said, holding his hand up to Sarah

as he knelt down to Tommy's level. "If you bring all of that, we're not going to fit in the tent, buddy. Besides, when you're camping you are roughing it. No toys, no TV, or computers. Just us, our sleeping bags, and the night."

"I can't bring any toys?" His lips curved downward, and Sarah watched as Cooper fell into Tommy's web.

"How about just one."

"Two, and we have a deal." Tommy held his hand out waiting for Cooper to shake it. Cooper hesitated for a second, pretending to ponder Tommy's negotiation.

"Deal," Cooper finally said and took Tommy's hand. "Now pick two and go put the rest back where they belong." Cooper rustled Tommy's hair again, and Tommy spun around.

"Yes, sir," he yelled as he took off.

"Wow," Cooper said, turning back to Sarah. "He really is your son."

"What is that supposed to mean?"

"He knows how to get what he wants."

"No, he just has you wrapped around his little finger."

Cooper cupped her face, stroking his thumb gently against the apple of her cheek. "Then that makes two of you." He kissed her softly and sweetly, but within seconds it turned desperate and raw.

She tried to control the carnal urges that flared up inside her, but with each slide of his tongue against hers, each gentle graze of his hand against her breast, she was having a hard time remembering why she wouldn't let him sleep over.

She was reminded as soon as she heard Tommy come into the kitchen. Before they could break apart Tommy cried out, "Eww."

Cooper laughed, but Sarah was absolutely mortified. She quickly brushed away the embarrassment and turned to the cabinets. "I'm thinking s'mores," she said.

***

The blush that crept up Sarah's neck and fanned out across her cheeks when Tommy discovered them was absolutely adorable. But as cute as it was, Cooper didn't want her to be uncomfortable in her own home because of him. He promised her while Tommy was around he would keep his distance, and that's what he planned to do.

It was going to be torture being in a small confined tent with her and not being able to touch her, but he would suffer to prove to her he was capable of honoring her wishes. He might not have liked the rules, but he understood them.

Especially now that there was a possibility he might be leaving on an eighteen-month trek across the Great Wall, he didn't want to give Tommy false hope. The kid was abandoned before he was born, and Cooper didn't want another male to let him down.

But who the hell was he fooling? He could sit there and pretend that by keeping his distance from Sarah that they were protecting Tommy, but at the end of the day it had nothing to do with the two of them. It had to do with the bond that he and Tommy had developed over the summer together.

Cooper didn't think he liked kids, but the truth was, he had more fun with Tommy than he did with people his own age. If only he could pack them up and bring them with him then he could have the best of both worlds. But not everybody's life was as restriction free and mobile as his. Tommy needed to go to school, and Sarah had a growing business to tend to. Not like she'd even agree to something if she didn't. Her life was all about structure and schedules, she wouldn't last a day out in the world with him since he rarely had a plan.

He turned back to her rising on tiptoes, her bare legs showing in a pair of linen shorts that were just short enough to tease him. For a moment, he just watched her as she went from one cabinet to the next, putting her calf muscles on display with each lift.

She placed all the ingredients on the counter. Tommy scooped them up, hugging the marshmallows close to his chest. "I'll bring these outside," he announced happily.

"Don't let me catch you sneaking them," Sarah said.

He came to a stop from running toward the door, spun around, and gave the world's biggest grin before taking off again.

"That smile means one thing," she said with a laugh as she turned toward him and rested her back against the counter. "Trouble. Are you sure you're prepared for tonight?"

Cooper beamed at her unable to take his eyes off of her as a million thoughts ran through his head.

"What's the matter?" Sarah asked, her eyebrows pinching tight in the middle.

I never want to leave you but I might. He couldn't say it. Being in a relationship, which he thought they were, meant sharing things, telling each other everything, yet the thought of telling Sarah that he might leave her for eighteen months gnawed at his gut.

He didn't want to talk about it, and he sure as hell was sick of thinking about it. He would figure it out. He always did. So he pushed the annoying dilemma to the back of his mind.

He snaked his hand around her waist and pressed a kiss to her neck, loving the soft feel and taste of her. Two things that he knew he could travel the world and never find such an intoxicating combination.

Sarah's hand brushed against his cheek, her fingers grabbing his chin and urging him to look into those beautiful dark eyes. "Talk to me. What's going on?"

He shook his head. "Just trying to figure out how I'm supposed to keep my hands to myself when we're going to be in such close quarters."

"Easy," she said with that adorable tilt of her lips. "It's called self-control." She patted his chest. "Learn some."

She went to walk away, but he grabbed her wrist, spinning her back to him. She let out a surprised yelp as she landed smack against his chest—exactly where he wanted her.

He ran his hand up and down her arm, needing to feel that soft skin against his. "Baby, the minute you walked into my life, I lost control."

"Ditto," she said, pushing up on her toes and giving him a chaste kiss. "But for tonight, for me, please try to keep your hands to yourself. I promise, I'll make it up to you."

He swallowed down the desire those words stirred inside him and tried not to focus on the heated look in her eyes. "Okay," he said, his voice gruffer than usual. "But I'm holding you to that." He kissed her one last time, long and hard before pulling away.

"I have a tent to put together," he said with a wink and disappeared outside, knowing damn well he left her breathless and wet.

Chapter 15

Cooper checked his email, hoping to hear from his agent and sadly disappointed when there wasn't a single word on his book. He had heard the publishing industry moved slowly, but this was pure torture. He shut out of his email, refusing to dwell on it, hoping no news meant good news and opened his Instagram account. He had a ton of new notifications. A lot for the pictures that made him famous—the ones where a monkey in Sri Lanka stole his camera right out of his hand and snapped a few pictures before he was able to get it back.

The pictures used to stir a desire inside him—make him want to jump on the next plane and discover something new and amazing that he knew a picture wouldn't be able to capture it as well as seeing it in person, but he would try anyway. Had to for his followers. Now as he looked at picture after picture the only thing he felt was dread.

Dread at the thought of leaving his family. At leaving Sarah and Tommy. At leaving his hometown that he always thought was too small and boring but now realized was quaint and welcoming. He'd spent seven years of his life refusing to settle down, and he swore he never would, and now he didn't know what he wanted.

He flipped over to the comment section on the throwback photo he posted yesterday and read the comments.

Great picture but when are you going somewhere new?
When are you coming to Chile?
You're hot.

Where have you been?
Anyone know what happened to him?
I love you. #boyfriendgoals
Sending my love from New Zealand. Please come here next!
He probably ran out of money.
Another recycled picture.

He tossed his phone on the counter and ran a hand over his face. The comment section used to make him feel like a million bucks. Now it just made him feel like a fraud, someone who'd let his passion and dreams fall to the realities of life. He was a dreamer. He never lived in reality; it was a place that never held enough for him until a stubborn, dark haired girl with an amazing mind and body walked into his life and knocked him on his ass.

A woman who knew exactly what she wanted out of life and didn't hesitate to make it happen. Who was fiercely independent and gave him a run for his money in a way no other woman had ever been able to do.

She didn't just knock him on his ass. She made him fall in love with her…

The only people he ever loved was his family. But even still this was different because no matter how much he loved his family, and he loved them a hell of a lot, they had never been enough to make him question giving up everything.

Last year, when Matt and Shay got married and then she got pregnant, it was enough to make him want to stay around for a little while. But he never planned on giving it all up. Not like he was thinking about now.

He had no idea what the hell he was going to do. All he knew was that it was five o'clock on a Saturday, and he needed to see Sarah. She and Gina took Tommy and Joey to the movies and then out for ice cream.

She hadn't been sure what time they'd be back, but Cooper didn't care. He would sit on her porch and wait for her. He needed to see her, even if it was just to quiet the unease and worry in his mind.

Fifteen minutes later, he pulled up into her driveway just as she was walking out the door, a vision in a white strapless dress that curved around her tits in two perfect arches and hit the perfect spot on her thigh that bordered on the line of not wanting her to be seen by any man but him.

"Hey, I was just on my way to your place."

"Really?" He couldn't stay away a second longer, taking long strides until his hands were in her hair and her lips pressed against his. A hunger took control of him as he tilted her head and deepened the kiss. Meeting him thrust for thrust she took whatever he threw at her and returned with as much passion.

He pulled away, not wanting to, but aware of where they were. "Where's Tommy?" he asked, glancing behind her, expecting the little man to be there.

"Staying at Joey's for the night."

A smile spread wide across his face as he grabbed her by the thighs and lifted her off the ground.

She cried out in a surprise. "What are you doing?"

"You have a lot of making up to do," he said against her breasts as he trailed his tongue across the beautiful mounds of flesh.

"I know," she said and reached down, grabbing his hand and moving it up her thigh. "Why do you think I was coming over?" She continued guiding his hand until he met the bare skin of her ass, gliding along the softness until his fingers brushed her wetness."

His dick hardened at the realization. "No panties?" he

asked a touch of amusement and wonder in his voice, but also red, hot desire.

Her teeth slid over her swollen bottom lip as she shook her head. Her eyes filled with raw burning want. "No panties."

In one sweeping move, he pushed the door opened and had it closed with her against it, his hands roaming the underside of her thighs.

He hadn't touched her like this since the night of their first date though he'd wanted to. God, had he wanted to, but she'd been sick and he wasn't an animal. But now that she was better, he couldn't hold back a second longer.

The need to be inside her consumed him, completely making him blind to everything else. He shoved his pants to the ground, taking his cock in hand and angling it toward her already wet folds. With one thrust he sunk in deep, her nails cutting into his shoulders as her head fell back against the door.

"Cooper," she cried, out and his name had never sounded so good.

He pumped in and out of her, forgetting any sense of romance and only focusing on the need to feel all of her. His teeth ripped her dress down, revealing her bare tits and causing him to thrust harder as he dipped his head, taking a pert nipple between his teeth. He gently nipped at the tight bud, and her body arched, allowing him to go even deeper inside her.

His tongue swirled and swiped at the beautiful light brown pearl before moving on to the next. Sarah's hands plunged into his hair, pulling and tugging at the strands as he continued to devour her.

A string of moans rose from her throat, slipping from

her sweet lips like music to his ears. Her muscles tightened around him and then her body began to shudder. He felt the pressure build inside him. He jumped on the wave, riding the crest, thrusting toward a release as she shattered around him. Her head fell against his neck, her hands holding him tight, and with one final thrust he followed her into sweet oblivion.

Seconds turned to minutes before he released her, letting her slide down his body.

"Oh fuck!" he said.

"What is it?"

"I got so caught up I forgot a condom." He never forgot a condom. Ever. The last thing he'd wanted was to be tied down by a kid. He'd always made sure to be safe.

"I'm on the pill," Sarah said.

"Oh, thank god," he muttered, resting his forehead against the wall beside her. "I'm clean. I was tested a while ago, and you're the only person I've been with since."

"I haven't had sex since I got pregnant."

"Wait. What?" Cooper pulled back, staring into her eyes. Sarah shifted as if his sudden attention made her uncomfortable. "You hadn't had sex in seven years?"

She shrugged as if it wasn't a big deal. "When you get pregnant the first time you have sex, it kind of puts a damper on things."

Cooper's mouth fell open at her admission. "Other than with me, you've only had sex one other time in your life?"

"Can you not make it a big deal? Because it's not."

She pulled her dress up over her tits and yanked the hem back into place. She was shutting down, ready to jump behind that aloof façade, but he wasn't about to let that happen.

He grabbed her waist, hauling her back to him and pinning her back against the wall. His arm rested above her head and his forehead mere inches from hers. "Don't walk away," he said.

"You're turning this into something."

"It kind of is something."

"No, it kind of isn't. It's not like I was a virgin mother."

"Why me?" he asked. Now that he knew this, he didn't understand of all the men in the world why she would choose him. Why after seven years she was ready for him.

"Because I didn't think you would make a big deal out of it."

He shook his head. "Try again. I'm not buying it."

She took a deep frustrated breath then met his eyes head on. He could see the underlying fear that sat just beneath the surface. He didn't want her to be scared to open up to him. He wanted her to be comfortable with him. And he thought she was, but if she couldn't confide in him maybe he was reading the whole situation wrong.

"People talk about butterflies. You know when you meet someone. This instant spark that is unexplainable yet undeniable. I never understood what that meant...until I met you."

"You too?" he said with a smile.

"You mean you've never...not once?"

"I've had chemistry and attraction with women but nothing like what we have. It's..."

"Scary as hell."

He laughed, loving her honesty. "Yeah."

"At least we agree on something," she said with a laugh.

He tucked her hair behind her ear and looked straight

into her dark brown eyes. She stared back at him sweet, innocent and everything he could have ever asked for. "I'm okay with scary as long as you are."

She nodded. "I am."

"Good." He kissed her forehead then her cheek. "Sarah."

"Yeah?"

"I think I've fallen in love with you."

She let out a slight laugh then met his gaze. "That's good because I think I've fallen in love with you, too."

"Really?" he asked, feeling the need for reassurance.

She nodded, assuring him completely. She wrapped her arms around his neck and kissed him. "I love you, Cooper Hayes. I didn't want to. Hell, I tried so hard not to, but I lost that fight. I love you."

"I love you too, baby," he said then swooped her off her feet and carried her straight to the bedroom, so he could not only tell her, but show her just how much he meant it.

***

Cooper had taken his time with her, loving every inch of her body. It was as if he was making up for all the years she had gone celibate, pleasuring her until she screamed his name over and over.

Now she rested, satiated and content against his chest, running her hand up and down the defined muscles of his abs.

She listened to the steady beat of his heart and relished in his warmth. She didn't want to think about the future, but now that she admitted to how she truly felt, it was all she could do.

Opening herself up, allowing to fall in love wasn't something that she planned, and now she didn't know how to navigate it. She had so many things to figure out. How did she tell Tommy? Did she tell Tommy? She knew Cooper wanted to be a part of her life, but did he want to be a part of Tommy's life, too? What did this do to her rule about sleeping over, because right now she couldn't imagine a single night without him in her bed, and the question that she didn't want to even think about and tried so desperately to push into hiding in the dark space in her mind—if it came down to it, would he choose his career over her?

He was a travel blogger; he wrote about his experiences travelling the globe. How much longer could he possibly stay before he had to set out again to gather new content? He had already been back in Red Maple Falls much longer than he had anticipated. At least that's what she had heard from Shay before they'd even got together.

His original intention was to leave after Shay had the baby but promised to be back by the baby's first birthday because he told Shay he didn't want to miss any milestones. The baby was here and so was Cooper; he hadn't left yet, but that didn't mean he wasn't going to. And she needed to plan for that. She needed to make sure she was prepared for whatever was to happen.

His hands wrapped around her waist, and he flipped her beneath him, knocking her out of her own thoughts. He kissed her forehead. "What's going on up here?" he asked, baby blue eyes staring down at her.

She could tell him about her fears. They could talk it out and figure things out together. He opened the door she just had to step through. But she didn't want to complicate things. Not yet. She wanted to enjoy the carefreeness of it just a little longer.

So instead of opening her hurt and voicing the thoughts

that were sure to keep her up at night, she reached up, running a finger across the bridge of his nose. "Where'd you get this scar?"

He kissed the side of her hand as she brought it down then smiled that ridiculously attractive smile. "My brother shot me."

Her eyes widened in terror. "*What*?"

He laughed. "It's not as bad as it sounds. It was a BB gun and the idiot forgot to turn the safety on. I got Mason back in the arm a year later."

"On purpose?"

"No, I was the idiot who forgot to turn the safety on that time."

"I have no idea how your mother did it."

"You should know. You're raising a little hell raiser yourself," Cooper said with a wink.

"I have one. She had three. Three boys and three girls. I couldn't even imagine. I have trouble keeping Tommy in line and keeping up with all of his schoolwork."

"Mom had help. She had Dad and Grandma and Grandpa. Matt and Kate helped out, too when they were old enough. She wasn't doing it alone. She had a whole village helping her."

"I had help in the beginning. My mom and dad were great. I don't know how I would've got through those first few years without them."

"Where are they now?"

"Right now, in the Philippines, visiting my mom's family. But the rest of the time they're back home in Connecticut."

"What made you come to Red Maple Falls?"

"My mom and my grandfather."

"The one who got you into jewelry making?"

She nodded, unable to get a reply out. Her grandfather was one of her favorite people and when he died it was as if a part of her died with him. "Once Tommy was born I spent all my time and energy focusing on him and what was best for him. My mom thought I should do something for myself. I always wanted to move away from home, travel the world, experience life, and then I got pregnant and never did. On my twenty-first birthday, she gave me a card that my grandfather had given her to give to me. Inside he wrote about how having a child will change your world, but don't forget about who you are. He wanted to see me happy. He said just because life didn't go the way I had planned didn't mean I couldn't go after the same dreams. He left me a decent chunk of money, but I wasn't allowed to put it away for Tommy. He already did that. This money was for me. So I decided it was time to leave home behind. Time to start fresh."

"At twenty-one you moved away—with a baby—from your support system?"

"I needed to prove to myself that I could do it on my own. That was important to me."

"Did you? Prove it yourself I mean?"

"I think so."

"You think so? You have an amazing kid and a thriving business. Whether you want to believe it or not, you're a success, baby."

"It does help that my kid is pretty amazing."

"He takes after his mom."

She swatted his chest. "You already got me in bed. You don't need to flatter me."

His lip quirked at the edge. "I'm not, I'm just telling it

as I see it. I mean, let's be honest. You have to be pretty amazing to snag a highly desirable guy, such as myself."

She responded with a tweak to his nipple that caused him to rear back with an amused smile and a surprised yelp.

"You shouldn't have done that," he said just as his fingers went to her sides and started tickling her.

He was relentless, and she kicked and squirmed all while laughing so hard it made her abs hurt. She couldn't remember the last time she laughed this hard. It felt good and free.

"Stop, stop!" she managed around the laughter.

Cooper pinned her hands above her head and smiled down at her. "All you had to do was ask."

"Jerk."

"Yes, but you love me anyway."

"God knows why," she said playfully.

His mouth dropped open in mock shock, and he pressed his growing erection at the apex of her thighs.

"I can think of one reason," he said with that sexy smirk.

"Trust me, that's not why I love you, but it does help."

He bit her lip then captured her mouth in an all-consuming kiss that sent heat rushing through her body.

He pulled back, looking down at her with those blue eyes. "How much does it help?"

"A lot." She reached up, taking his face in her hands and pulling him toward her. "Now get back here."

"Whatever you want, baby. Whatever you want."

She looked into the depths of his clear blue eyes as if she could see straight through to his soul and murmured, "I want you to make love to me."

And he did. He kissed and worshipped every part of

her body and when he finally entered her, the connection she felt was so profound that she couldn't tell where his body began and hers ended. As one together, he continued to move in and out of her till her walls clenched around him.

"I love you," she cried out as she fell into a blinding powerful freefall that left her breathless, completely sated and more in love with him than she ever could have imagined.

Chapter 16

Tick Tock.

Cooper stared down at the text from Gray. A reminder that each day that past was one less day he had to make a decision. July had somehow melted into August, and before he knew it, it would be September. He was running out of time. He needed to decide, but how the hell was he supposed to decide between two parts of his heart?

Trekking across the Great Wall was an opportunity of a lifetime. He wasn't getting any younger, and if there was ever a time to do something it was now. He had the money, he had the time, and his fans were getting restless with his recycled posts.

His platform was what made him. They were the reason he had money and time. If he said yes, he wasn't only saying yes to Gray, he was saying yes to his one point five million followers. He needed to give them something new to see because he had a feeling the moose expedition he took a group of seven-year-olds on the other day wasn't going to cut it, even if Kyle had said it was awesome—a declaration that made him happier than he'd expected.

But on the other side of his heart sat Sarah and Tommy. How the hell was he supposed to up and leave them for eighteen months? He didn't like when a day went by when he didn't see Sarah's beautiful smile or hear Tommy's contagious laugh.

He promised Sarah he wouldn't disappoint Tommy, and he wouldn't. If he did decide to go, he would explain to

Tommy about how it was a once in a lifetime experience. Promise to call, video chat, and email every day.

Somehow, he didn't think it would be enough. And that was where the problem lay.

He let his head fall into his hands as the debate raged on in his mind. Finally, fed up and in desperate need of advice, he grabbed his keys and headed out to the one person he always counted on when he couldn't make a decision.

Ten minutes later, he pulled up to Five Leaf Brewery and threw the truck in park. He hopped out and headed in, hoping that Mason wouldn't be too busy. Even if he was, Cooper knew he'd drop everything for him if he asked him to.

He walked in and spotted Cassie behind the bar, filling a tasting glass for a flight. Her reddish-brown hair fell across her eyes as she looked down at the pour. She looked up, shaking her hair back into place and handing the wooden flight board to the customer.

She smiled at the guy then spotted Cooper and gave him a wave as he made his way over to her.

Before he sat down he leaned over the bar and gave her a kiss on the cheek. There was a time when she didn't even like to be hugged, not that he could blame her after everything she had been through, but now she was as much a part of the Hayes family as the rest of them. It took time, but the shy, timid girl that Mason picked up on the side of the road was gone, and in her place was a witty, fun loving woman who absolutely adored his brother. Cooper couldn't be happier for either of them.

"You look like you could use a beer," she said, grabbing a glass and filling it with his favorite: the Hippidy Hop IPA.

"You have no idea."

He looked around the brewery, still amazed at how it turned out. When Cooper first came home and Mason showed him this place, Cooper was skeptical. But Mason had a vision and he didn't stop until it came to fruition. If anything, the brewery exceeded his vision and became his ultimate master piece.

The place was beautiful, refurbished but keeping that rustic feel that Red Maple Falls was all about. The two crates Cooper had picked up at Sophie's place were sitting on a table on their side, displaying brewery merchandise.

Cassie slid the glass across the bar, and Cooper gratefully picked it up, taking a long sip.

"Where's your other half?" Cooper asked as he placed the glass back down.

"In the back changing out one of the kegs. He should be up here soon. Anything I can help you with?" she asked.

He thought about asking Cassie, lay it all out there, tell her about Sarah and Tommy, about Gray and the Great Wall. It would be good to have a female perspective, and he was about to open up when he heard Mason come up behind him.

"You look like shit," he said to Cooper then leaned over the bar and gave his girl a kiss.

"Keg is all set."

"Just in time for the crowd," Cassie said, her eyes on the door.

Cooper and Mason turned just as a bunch of people walked through the door.

"Let me just help her out," Mason said but Cassie waved her hand at him.

"Nope, I got this. You two go talk. Coop looks like he

needs an ear."

"You sure?" Mason asked, looking at her in a way that made Cooper think he could read exactly what she was thinking beyond the words that came out of her mouth.

"I'm good."

"We're just going to be upstairs. Call up if you need me."

"Will do," she said then turned to the crowd, handing out tasting menus and diving right into an explanation of how the tasting room worked.

Cooper waited for Mason to grab a beer and top Cooper's glass off then he followed him upstairs to his apartment.

Inside was spotless except for a few things of Cassie's that were scattered around. "You two moving in together yet?" Cooper asked.

Mason let out a sigh, placed his beer on the kitchen island, and sat down on a stool. "No," he said, and Cooper detected disappointment in his tone. "She said she wants more time."

"Guessing you're not too happy about that?"

Mason ran a hand over his face, leaned forward, and rested his elbows on the island. "I get it. I do. After everything she went through she needed to prove to herself that she could do things on her own. But it's been months now. I guess I'm just getting impatient."

"By the looks of it, she stays here a lot."

"She does, and when she's not here I'm at her place."

"So you're practically living together already."

"I know. I just want to make it official."

A few months ago, Cooper would've told Mason to hang on to his independence as long as he could. Why rush it? But now, he understood wanting to be with someone so badly that you were willing to sacrifice not only where you lived and how you lived but your independence.

He wanted that. For the first time in his life he didn't want to take off at the first opportunity. He wanted to stay and see where this thing between him and Sarah was headed.

"Enough about me," Mason said. "What's going on?"

Cooper smiled, his answers had been inside of him all along. He just needed to open his eyes to see them. "Nothing," Cooper said. "Nothing at all. Just wanted to come say hi and drink your beer."

Mason was always the one Cooper went to whenever he needed advice, someone to listen while he talked shit out and tried to make sense of whatever it was. Mason was the listener in their family, and it wasn't until that moment that Cooper realized Mason had listened to him time and time again yet Cooper rarely returned the favor. Maybe Mason didn't have much to talk about, or maybe he didn't think he had anyone who would want to listen.

Cooper took a sip of his beer then nodded to Mason.

"Let's talk more about you."

***

It was Thursday, but Sarah's craving for a blueberry muffin was so intense she couldn't ignore it no matter how hard she tried. So she took the fifteen minute drive into town to make a special stop at Sweet Dreams Bakery.

When she walked in the door the first thing she noticed was Shay behind the counter.

"Welcome back," Sarah said as she approached the counter.

"Sarah!" Shay said with a smile that fell almost instantly. "Oh my god, it's Monday? I thought it was Thursday. I'm losing my mind."

Sarah quickly held up her hand and shook her head, trying not to laugh at the memories of being sleep deprived. "No, you're right. It's Thursday."

"Oh, thank heavens," Shay said as she rested against the back counter in relief. "I honestly thought I had lost it."

"My fault. I only ever come in on a Monday."

"It is your fault," Shay said with a smile. "So what brings you in today?"

"A blueberry muffin craving. Tried to ignore it and I can't. I must be PMSing."

"I used to think PMSing was the worst thing in the world, but man. Nothing compares to the crap you go through after you have the baby. My hormones are all over the place. One minute I'm laughing and the next I'm crying. I'm surprised Matt hasn't had me committed."

"Your body is adjusting. You'll be back to normal before you know it."

"I don't even remember what normal is."

Sarah laughed. "Somewhere between delusional and drunk."

"I would kill for a glass of wine."

"So why not have one?"

"I'm breastfeeding, and I know I can pump beforehand but I'm so scared about doing permanent damage and I know the chances are slim to none but my parents messed me up without alcohol and I promised I would never hurt my child so here I am, suppressing my wine craving with chocolate. At this rate, I'll never lose the baby weight."

Some days it felt like yesterday when Sarah had Tommy and other days it felt like an eternity. Alcohol was never an issue for her since she wasn't of age to drink even if she wanted to. She remembered the onslaught of confusing emotions and the desperate desire to lose the baby weight. It had been so long since she had thought about those things, and now that she did, she remembered how horrible it could be.

Everyone tells you having a baby is the greatest thing you'll ever do, but they forget to tell you all the changes your body endures and how you don't jump right back into shape as soon as the baby is out. It takes time and work.

Luckily, Sarah had been young and people told her that made it easier for her. She imagined it did. It had been weeks since she had the flu, yet she felt like she still wasn't a hundred percent.

"Hang in there," she said to Shay. "You're doing great."

Shay's eyes softened. "Thanks." She let out a breath and turned to the display case. "One blueberry muffin coming right up. Then you're going to eat it here, I don't care if you have to get back to work, and tell me all about you and my brother-in-law."

"There's nothing to tell," Sarah said, but couldn't keep the silly grin from taking over her face.

"Uh huh. That's exactly what I thought."

Shay placed the muffin on a plate and grabbed a chocolate cupcake for herself. They walked over to a table in the corner after Shay yelled in the back to Louise that she was taking a breather.

"So?" Shay said, forking a piece of cupcake.

"So what?"

"Oh, don't play coy with me. I hear Cooper is bringing you and Tommy to Sunday dinner. I didn't realize it was so serious."

"It's not."

"Does Cooper know this?"

"I mean. We're taking each day at a time. With his job, I know it's only a matter of time before he has to leave, so we're just enjoying each other's company right now."

"It's okay to want more," Shay said her voice sympathetic. "But you're right. His job takes him away for long periods of time to places where he's unable to be reached. Have you guys talked about it?"

"Not really. Like I said we're living in the now. Not worrying about the future." The more she said it the less and less she was actually believing it.

Shay looked skeptical as she poked at her cupcake.

"What?"

"You can't hide from the future. It comes whether you want it to or not."

"I know."

Shay reached across the table and rested her hand on hers. "You can't stop it but you can prepare for it."

Shay was absolutely right. Sarah wanted to live in the now and not worry about what was to come but you could only live in the moment for so long before it became the past and the present turned into the future. She needed to protect herself and her heart for when the time came for Cooper to take off.

"Now that's out of the way, I figured I'd be a good friend and give you some pointers for Sunday night dinner."

Sarah raised a curious eyebrow. "Pointers? It's just dinner."

Shay let out a loud laugh and slapped a hand over her mouth. "Just dinner. Have you met Betty Hayes?"

"I have. She's a sweetheart."

"If you mean a sweetheart with no filter, a dirty mind,

and the determination to marry off all her grandchildren and have them reproducing the next generation then you have her pinned."

Sarah's eyes widened at Shay's description. She took a generous bite of her muffin then settled back into her seat. "Okay, I'm listening."

Chapter 17

In all of his twenty-six years, Cooper never brought home a girl, especially not for Sunday night dinner. Having a date for Sunday night dinner was admitting to, not just yourself, but to your family that you were in a committed relationship. The closest thing Cooper ever had to a committed relationship was owning the same backpack for three years. Other than that, everything in Cooper's life was temporary. At least until Sarah.

Most of his family knew her from town, but he wanted them to officially meet her as his girlfriend. He felt almost juvenile, needing his family's approval, but he wanted them to love her as much as he did. It was important to him.

Sarah and Tommy met him at his place, and Sarah handed him a bottle of wine. "For me?" he asked.

"No, it's for your mother. I figured it was pointless to bring dessert since Shay will be here, and beer was out of the question because I'm sure Mason keeps them stocked, so wine it is. Unless someone in your family owns a winery that I don't know about."

"As of right now no, but never say never."

"All I care about is right now," Sarah said then gave him a kiss hello on the cheek as Tommy stared up at Cooper's house.

"It's like a treehouse but bigger and not in a tree," Tommy said.

"Cooper ruffled his hair and laughed. "That's a good way to describe it. I'll give you a tour later when we get back."

Cooper took Sarah's hand in his, happy she was finally letting him be affectionate to her in front of Tommy, and started on their way to the main house. Tommy ran ahead but turned back every so often to make sure they were keeping up.

Just as he was about to turn the corner toward the house, Lady, Hadley's dog, a golden Cocker Spaniel came around the bend.

"Look, Mom! It's a dog."

"That is Lady," Hadley in a pair of cut off shorts and a t-shirt said as she walked toward Tommy.

"Can I pet her?"

"Of course you can. Just be gentle; she's an old dog."

Hadley had adopted Lady after fostering her and falling in love with her. The two had been inseparable ever since.

Tommy dropped to his knees and ran his hand over Lady's head.

"Hadley, you know Sarah Kramer?" Cooper said.

"I do. It's a pleasure to see you. Have no idea what you're doing with this doofus, though."

"He grows on you," Sarah said, turning to Cooper and giving him a wink.

"Like a fungus."

"Hads, don't you have something to be doing?"

"Yup, looking for you. It's a minute after five. Mom sent the search party out."

"Oh no, are we late?" Sarah asked, checking her watch. "I knew I should've picked up the wine yesterday and not have waited until today."

"It's fine," Hadley assured her. "Besides, our family is used to waiting on Cooper." Hadley gave him a sassy smirk then bent down to Tommy and Lady.

"Do you like animals, Tommy?"

"I love animals. But Mom won't let me get a dog."

"They're a lot of responsibility. I have Lady, but I also take care of other dogs, too. It's a lot of work."

"Like how much work?"

"Well, you have to feed them and walk them and bathe them and make sure you give them all the love." Hadley pulled Lady close and kissed her snout. "Dogs like to be spoiled, and I think they should be. If you think you can handle all of that then I think you're ready for a dog."

"Hadley," Cooper warned. "Stop trying to color the world with dogs."

"Maybe you should get a dog. Show you a little responsibility."

Cooper turned to Sarah and shook his head. "She's been trying to get me to adopt a dog for years. She doesn't realize how hard it would be to travel with a dog. It's not like another human."

"Maybe it's not such a bad idea. I mean, you don't have anything planned for a while, right?" Sarah said, and Cooper couldn't help but think she was insinuating something without actually saying it.

He ran a hand through his hair, not wanting to have this conversation right now or right here in front of an audience. He didn't have anything planned, but he wanted to talk about his future, their future, in private.

"Coop, if you get a dog, it'll be like *I* have a dog, since you're over all the time," Tommy said.

Hadley tilted her eyebrow up and glanced toward Cooper. Everyone in the Hayes family knew Cooper and Sarah were dating, but he didn't think they knew how serious it actually was. If they didn't, Hadley did now and they would soon find out, too.

"We need to get to the house before Mom sends out someone to find Hadley," Cooper said, walking toward the house and hopefully leaving the conversation in the dust.

At the house, everyone welcomed Sarah and Tommy with open arms and warm smiles. Betty Hayes couldn't wait to pinch Tommy's cheek which he wasn't a big fan of but appeased the old woman.

The girls swooped Sarah up in conversation and Tommy was telling Betty and Harold everything he had learned at camp this summer. Cooper stood back, listening to Tommy with pride. Thrilled that the things he taught the kid actually stuck with him. He wondered what else he would teach him and if they were things that would help him become a better man, better person.

Cooper felt a strong hand land on his shoulder, and he didn't need to look to know it was his father. "He seems like a good kid," Jonathon Hayes said and hearing that was as if Jonathon was giving him a compliment which was ridiculous since he had nothing to do with who Tommy was, though, he hoped that he would one day.

"He is," Cooper replied. "Smart as hell, too. Loves a good adventure."

Jonathon squeezed Cooper's shoulder. "Sounds like someone I know." Jonathon looked out to the farm then back at Cooper. "It's nice having you home. I don't know if I've said that before."

He hadn't, but it's not like Cooper was keeping tabs on who did. It was nice to hear all the same.

"I just hope this means you finally found what you were looking for." Jonathon patted him on the back and walked away, leaving Cooper confused.

He hadn't been looking for anything other than the next country, the next adventure.

While Cooper contemplated what his dad said he turned and caught a glimpse of Sarah who was laughing at something Kate said. She looked absolutely radiant with her long dark hair hanging in loose waves, her face practically glowing beneath the afternoon sun seeping in through the skylights.

Maybe he was looking for something this whole time and didn't even realize it. He had gone from country to country, wandering the world with no purpose other than to find his next big adventure. Maybe all this time what he was looking for was an anchor—someone to make him want to stop moving. Someone who would hold onto him long enough to make him realize everything he could ever want was right in front of him if he would just take a minute to absorb it all in.

Sarah was his anchor. She didn't just keep him grounded; she opened his eyes to what he always knew but could never seem to see.

There was absolutely no place like home.

He took out his phone and typed a quick message to Gray.

Call me. We need to talk about China.

Mason walked over with an extra beer in hand, and Cooper put his phone on the table as he accepted the glass.

Cooper raised his glass to Mason's then took a sip, grateful for the good food, the good beer, and the love of his family.

***

Sarah knew most of Cooper's family, but being surrounded by them all at once, in their home, there was nothing like it.

It reminded her of summers at her grandparents in the Philippines, something she had missed and cherished deeply. She had always wanted Tommy to be able to experience the love of family and friends gathering together, being a part of such a big group of people and knowing that no matter what there would be laughs, love, and good food.

Even if Tommy only got to experience it this one time, she was grateful because the smile on his face while he told any Hayes who would listen, which was practically all of them, about his camp adventures was heart-warming. It also made her realize that she needed to plan a trip home.

Her parents visited twice a year, and Sarah was okay with that because she was so adamant to prove she could raise Tommy on her own. But the truth was, she was only hurting him by not allowing his grandparents to be a big part of his life. And also, maybe it was time her and Tommy took a trip to visit the family he had never met.

Like Cooper had said, it took a village to raise him and his siblings, and Sarah loved how close they all were to not only their parents but their grandparents. Tommy deserved that.

By trying to be the best mom and showing him how to be independent she wasn't doing him any favors. She was denying him a massive support system.

She made a mental note to call her parents tomorrow.

"That son of yours is a riot," Betty Hayes said, coming up beside her.

"I hope he's not too much,"

"Oh, poppy cock. He's absolutely delightful."

Sarah breathed a breath of relief.

"I miss having kids around. All my grandbabies are all grown now, so it's nice to have him here with baby Matthew.

The next generation. I hope you both will be coming around more often. Maybe add to the kiddie pool."

If Shay hadn't prepared Sarah she might have choked on her lemonade. Instead, she didn't miss a beat as she looked Betty straight in her blue eyes and smiled.

"Cooper and I are taking things slow. Tommy's more than I could have ever asked for. I don't plan on having any more."

Betty's lips drooped into a straight line before she burst out with a loud ear piercing laugh. "If that isn't the biggest lie I've ever heard."

"I'm not lying," Sarah said.

"If you're not lying to me then you're lying to yourself, sweetie."

Sarah knew this was just one of Betty's mind games, so she shook her head, determined to stay adamant. "Honestly, I'm not."

Betty patted her hand as if she felt bad for her. "I see how you look at him."

"What does that have to do with anything?"

"You don't look at someone like that unless you want to have their babies."

Sarah went to reply, but the words got stuck somewhere between her throat and her lips and before she could manage to get them out Betty Hayes left her to move on to her next victim.

She felt bad for poor Kate, but was grateful for the moment alone.

A few moment later, Cooper wrapped his arms around her stomach, his chin resting on her shoulder. "What were you and my grandma talking about?"

"You don't want to know."

"You're probably right," Cooper said with a laugh. "Just don't take anything she says to heart. She means well, but sometimes she goes a little overboard."

Sarah turned in his arms until she was looking into his eyes. "Nothing she can say can scare me off. Besides, Shay warned me already so I was prepared."

Cooper laughed. "I bet Grandma didn't expect the forces to work against her."

Sarah held her finger over her lips. "Shh. What she doesn't know can't hurt her."

"Your secret is safe with me."

"Thank you," Sarah said, followed by a yawn.

"Tired?"

"I shouldn't be, but I am."

Cooper brushed her hair behind her ear. "You feeling okay?"

"Just tired."

"Let's get you home then."

"Coop?"

"Yeah, baby?"

She shrugged, trying not to make it a big deal. "Maybe… you could spend the night."

An adorable smile touched the corners of his mouth. "Do I have to keep my hands to myself?"

She bit her lip, a hot rush of desire rushing through her body and straight to her core. "Not if you can be quiet about it."

"Oh, baby, I'm not the one who's going to have to be quiet."

He kissed her just long enough to insinuate what was to come then pulled away, leaving her desperate to get him home and alone.

Chapter 18

Sarah sat on the table, drumming her hands against the paper. Time felt like it was at a standstill, and she'd be sitting in that room for the rest of eternity. She checked the time on her cell phone for the hundredth time and was discouraged to see only two minutes had passed since the last check.

She had a million things to tackle on her to-do list and couldn't put them off. Still, her health was important. She had lost so much time the last time she got sick, and she was terrified of that happening again. It was bothering her that she wasn't feeling a hundred percent and just wanted to get checked out to let her know she was on the mend instead of harboring something that could potentially take her out for another week.

Finally, there was a slight knock on the door as it eased opened. The doctor stepped in, donning a long white lab coat and a smile.

"Mrs. Kramer."

"Miss," she corrected him.

"My apologies. I guess congratulations are in order."

"Excuse me?"

Confused, Sarah narrowed her gaze at the doctor.

"You're pregnant."

A laugh bubbled up and flew out. If that wasn't the most absurd thing she had ever heard. "You must have the wrong room. I'm Sarah Kramer. I'm just here for a routine check-up."

The doctor looked down at his chart. "No, I have the

right room. If I had to guess you're about four weeks along."

Pregnant.

The words were like a swift kick to the gut, knocking the wind right out of her.

No. This couldn't be happening. Not again. The room spun and blurred around her. Her hands tightened on the edge of the table, the white paper crinkling beneath her grip. "No," she said, meant for no one but herself as she rocked back and forth, trying to make sense of it all. "I'm on the pill. I don't understand."

She glanced up, her eyes catching the doctor's, searching for a different answer but knowing there wasn't one. She was pregnant. Again. And just like before, it wasn't planned. How in the world was she going to tell Cooper? He told her on that first date that he wasn't the settling down type. He didn't do relationships. She couldn't just spring this on him. She wasn't naïve. A baby wasn't going to change someone like Cooper. He was set in his ways, a free-spirit, just waiting to move on to the next big adventure. All she was to him was a pit stop on his never-ending train to nowhere. She knew that. Accepted it. But this changed things.

She had finally gotten her life together—a career she loved, a town filled with people she adored, Tommy who was thriving and happy. Oh god. How was she going to explain this to Tommy?

Things just got real in a way she wasn't prepared for. Control was stripped away from her, and there was nothing she could do. She swallowed down the panic, trying not to think about diapers and bottles and middle of the night feedings, but how could she not focus on those things?

It was like she was reliving it all over again. This

couldn't be happening. She refused to believe it.

Dr. Steinman sat down on his stool, rolling closer to her. "You said you had been sick. I'm assuming you were taking something."

"Yes. Of course. I mean I had the flu and an upper respiratory infection. I had no choice. I was on antibiotics."

"Unfortunately, antibiotics can counteract the pill. We always tell our patients to use condoms for at least a week after just to be safe."

She shook her head. "No one told me. Why wouldn't they tell me?"

"It's on the packaging."

"Nobody reads the packaging." Panic rose in her voice as she slouched back onto the table, trying to calm herself down.

The doctor's head tilted for a moment then he let out a breath. "No, but they should."

There was no use in continuing this discussion. What was done was done. She was pregnant. Pregnant. Maybe if she kept saying it over and over in her head she'd finally be able to grasp it. Find a way to make sense of it all.

It dawned on her then that it might not have even been the antibiotic, she had missed a day of her pills, but she doubled up when she emerged from her sick bed.

Dr. Steinman was still talking, but she had stopped listening. There was nothing he could tell her that she didn't already know.

So many people would feel blessed knowing they were expecting, and she felt guilty for the shock and fear that was consuming her. She took a deep breath, forcing down the panic and channeling the courage that lay inside her.

She was scared once before, terrified actually, and now

she couldn't imagine her life without Tommy. Her life had always been about making the impossible possible, and this wasn't going to change that. If anything, it was only going to reinforce it.

"Are you going to be okay? Do you need me to call someone?" the doctor asked. "The father maybe."

"No!" she blurted then cleared her throat. God, she could only imagine how that call would go. "I mean. No. I'm okay." The last thing she needed was a doctor calling Cooper. She would deal with that bridge when she got to it. Right now, she wanted to take the low road and avoid that route until she had a plan. She was good at making plans, at figuring things out. Once she had this all mapped out she would tell him, and maybe knowing that she had it figured out it would lessen the shock. Put his mind at ease that she had everything under control.

"If you have any questions…"

"I think I'm good."

"I'll see you soon, then," Dr. Steinman said before walking out and leaving her alone with the bombshell he just dropped on her.

Soon. She thought about all the doctor appointments she would have to work into her schedule. All the items she would need to buy so she could prepare for this unexpected arrival. She had so much to do, and she had no idea where she was even going to start.

It was too early to know what she was having, so she couldn't buy clothes unless she bought everything in yellow. Would it be a boy or a girl? She imagined a blue-eyed boy with golden brown hair and a mischievous smile looking back at her. A baby girl with the same blue eyes lined with long, beautiful lashes.

She rested her hand on her stomach, the slightest of smiles playing at the corner of her lips. Whether Cooper wanted to be a part of this child's life, it didn't matter.

All that mattered was this kid would be loved. She would make sure of it.

Chapter 19

Cooper's phone buzzed in his pocket for the nine hundredth time, and he let out a sigh as he reached for it. Gray's name flashed on his screen again. Ever since he told Gray he couldn't go to China the texts hadn't stopped. Gray was determined to convince Cooper that he was making a big mistake.

Cooper already made up his mind and nothing would change that. For the first time in his life, he made a decision that he was absolutely certain about. He loved Sarah, there was no denying that now, and he couldn't imagine a day, no less five-hundred-and-forty-seven and a half days apart from her.

It's going to be epic. I'll see you in September.

No, he wouldn't. Cooper shoved his phone back in his pocket and ignored Gray. He hoped by ignoring him he would stop with the texts and give up.

He slid out of his truck and headed up to Sarah's door. She hadn't answered his phone when he called but assumed she was still at the doctor's. He thought he'd hang out until she got home but was surprised when he pulled up and her car was in the driveway.

She was probably consumed in work. He knocked on the door and was about to let himself in when the door flew open and Tommy bounced out.

"Coop! You're here," he said and flung his arms around his waist as if it was the most natural thing to do. He let go almost as quickly, but the effects of the affectionate move still lingered. "Come on, I want to show you something!" Tommy announced and ran back in the house.

Cooper cleared his throat, swallowing down the unexpected emotion and followed Tommy to his room.

"Look! Look!" Tommy's voice got louder and louder as Cooper turned into the room. He pointed to the floor where he had constructed an entire village out of Legos.

"Wow, buddy. This is awesome!"

Cooper got down on his knees to get a closer look at Tommy's masterpiece.

"This is the post office," he pointed to the left. "Then this is Sweet Dreams Bakery and this is your parents' farm." He moved his hand through the Lego town and stopped at a very small building. "And this is your house."

There were three Lego people and a dog placed on a path he made leading to the house. "And who are these people?" Cooper asked.

"That's me, Mom, and you, duh. Oh, and this is our dog."

Cooper smiled. He knew for so long that Sarah and Tommy was an unbreakable unit and somehow for whatever reason this amazing kid accepted him into it. He had no idea what he did to deserve it, but he was grateful.

"I thought your Mom said you weren't getting a dog."

"I know, but she also said I wasn't getting a dad either but…" He shrugged then met Cooper's eyes with those innocent brown ones. "I did."

That same emotion from earlier rose in his throat, and he did his best to keep it at bay, but it was getting harder and harder to control it. Tears pricked the back of his eyes and his throat burned. He wasn't an emotional person, was always the one who could brush things off, yet a seven-year-old boy with big brown eyes and freckles was making him break. And it wasn't just because it was unexpected, which it was. No, it was so much more than that.

He was…honored.

A few months ago, the thought of being anyone's dad would have had him running for the hills, but now he wanted to make sure he did everything to make this kid proud of him.

Cooper smiled. "I'll see what I can do about the dog."

Tommy's eyes doubled inside. "Really?"

"Really. But no promises."

Tommy tackled Cooper in a hug, and Cooper laughed. Just as he looked up he spotted Sarah looking down at them from the doorway. A sad smile touched her lips, and he quickly play wrestled Tommy off of him, setting him on the floor while Cooper stood.

"Hey baby," Cooper said, cupping her cheek. "Everything okay?"

She nodded and smiled. "Everything's good."

He narrowed his eyes, not believing her for a second. "What aren't you telling me?"

"Nothing."

Dread landed in his stomach like a solid mass. "How was the doctor?" She tired-out easily lately and while they both assumed it was after effects of the flu maybe it wasn't. Oh god, what if it was something worse?

What if she was really sick?

No. That was impossible. He wouldn't believe it. But the world had a funny way of throwing him curve balls so he needed to be sure.

"Please tell me everything's okay."

She met his eyes and though her lips weren't smiling

her beautiful brown eyes were. "Everything is fine."

"Oh, thank god." He rested his forehead against hers as relief flooded him. "Go get your purse," he said.

"Why?"

"Because," Cooper said with a smile, "we're going out to celebrate."

"Celebrate what?"

His lip quirked, and the joy that he'd been holding inside of him burst out of him. "My agent called today. There's been an offer on my book."

"Are you serious?" Sarah asked the smile on her lips finally genuine.

"As a heart attack."

He scooped her up in his arms and swung her around when he placed her back on the ground she took his face in her hands.

"Oh my god! How are you just telling me this now?"

"I tried calling, but you didn't answer."

"I must've left my phone in the car."

"It's okay. I'd rather have told you in person anyway."

He kissed her long and hard until Tommy made several noises of disgust. He pulled back with a laugh. "Come on Tommy. Go get cleaned up. I'm buying you the biggest dessert on the menu tonight."

"With hot fudge and sprinkles?"

"You know it."

"Wahoo!" Tommy yelled as he jumped up and ran down the hallway.

Cooper turned back to Sarah who seemed to be somewhere else entirely. "Are you sure you're okay?" he asked, needing reassurance.

She patted his chest then lifted up on tiptoe and kissed

him. "I'm just so proud of you," she said. "Let's go celebrate."

She took him by the hand and led him toward the front door, but he couldn't shake the feeling that she was hiding something from him.

***

All day Sarah had been wrestling with whether to tell Cooper or not that she was pregnant. *Pregnant.* She thought she'd get used to the word if she said it enough, but it was just as shocking now as it was the first time.

She had finally decided to hold off for a little bit when she overheard Cooper and Tommy talking. Tommy called him "Dad" and maybe it was in an indirect way the intent was still there. Sarah had choked up in the hallway and needed a second to get herself together.

She waited to hear Cooper's response, wondering how he would handle it. He was notorious for taking off, and she waited, expecting him to make some lame excuse and go flying out of the room, and when he didn't, warmth rushed through her body filling her heart.

When she stepped in and saw the two loves of her life in an embrace, she had made up her mind. She was going to tell him. She only hoped that it wouldn't be too much too soon because her biggest fear was him leaving her to be a single mom again.

Cooper treated them to dinner at the Happy Apple where Terry and Walt joined them for a few moments to help toast Cooper's success. After Tommy had his massive dessert Cooper had promised him, they headed home.

Tommy was fast asleep in the backseat and Cooper's hand inched higher and higher up her thigh. "Remember the last time we went out to dinner."

"Tommy is in the backseat. I don't care if he's sleeping. Don't you get any ideas."

"Oh, I have ideas all right, but don't worry. I don't plan on acting on them until Tommy is in bed, and we're behind closed doors."

The thought of Cooper's hands on her, his mouth exploring her body caused moisture to pool between her legs. Even though she was exhausted, she couldn't wait to get home.

They pulled into the driveway a few minutes later, and Sarah went to get Tommy out of the backseat when Cooper rested his hand on her shoulder. "I got him. You go ahead in."

"You sure?" she asked, and Cooper nodded. "Okay."

She went to the front door and opened it before turning back and watched Cooper carry Tommy from the car.

He walked by pressing his finger to his lip as he passed. She followed behind, easing the door shut quietly and heading to her bedroom.

She slipped into a black silk night gown and waited for Cooper who didn't make her wait long. He paused in the doorway, leaning against the frame as he filled the small space. His gaze roamed up and down her body with a hunger radiating from his eyes.

Her teeth slid over her bottom lip and she shifted causing the silky material to rub against her most intimate parts. "Like what you see?" she asked.

"You have no idea how much."

"Then come show me." She beckoned him with her finger and watched as he stalked across the room, pulling his shirt over his head as he moved.

She knew she should tell him about the baby, but just in case it was too much for him, and he walked away from her, she wanted this moment. She wanted to feel him inside her, to wrap her legs around him and stare into the blue depths of his eyes while he brought her to the edge. She needed something to hold onto.

His hand snaked around her waist, and he yanked her toward him, bringing them skin to silk. She ran a hand up his abdomen to his chest, branding every solid curve and cut line to memory. In her heart, she wanted to believe that she didn't need to. That Cooper wasn't going anywhere, but her heart had failed her before, and she needed to listen to her head.

He took her hand and brought it to his lips, kissing each fingertip before backing her toward the bed. The back of her knees hit the mattress, and she fell back just as he lowered himself on top of her.

His eyes bore into hers, holding an intensity that was much stronger than ever before. Or maybe it was just her hoping it was, searching for a glimmer of reassurance that he was in as deep as she was.

She tilted her head, capturing his lips with hers, and pulling him down to her. A battle broke out in her mind between needing him now and making it last as long as she could, but the need for him was too strong to deny.

"I need you," she said against his mouth. "Don't make me wait."

She reached down and lifted up, removing her night gown and tossing it to the floor.

"Please," she begged.

He reached for a condom, and she wrapped her hand around his. She shook her head as she pulled his hand away.

"I need to feel all of you. No barriers," she said, looking into his eyes and showing him how desperately she needed this.

His other hand tightened around her waist, dragging her closer to him. He swiped a finger across her slick folds, moaning.

"I love how ready you are for me," he said, pressing the tip of his erection at her wet entrance.

"Always," she said, and he pushed into her causing her to gasp at the delicious intrusion.

Her hands tightened around his neck, and he smiled down at her. "That's right. Hold on, baby. Things are about to get crazy."

He had absolutely no idea just how crazy things were going to get, but she heeded his request and held on with all that she had because she had no idea how the night was going to end.

She sent up a silent prayer then let all the fears dissipate as she focused on just feeling. His lips came down on her, sucking and nipping at her. His tongue swirled around her nipple before he moved to the next.

Cold and hot mixed together sending heated desire and intense chills to every inch of her body. His hands wrapped around her back and next thing she knew they were on the edge of the bed with her on top.

She moved against him, tightening her legs around his back and pulling their slick bodies closer together. His fingers laced through her hair, moving it aside as his mouth kissed a fiery path up her neck.

Tiny sparks began to glimmer when his thumb pressed against her swollen nub. He moved his thumb in mind-numbing circles until the tiny sparks ignited an inferno, sending her spiraling to no return.

Her body bucked against him, but he didn't stop his ministrations and just when she thought the wave was about to crash to an end his hands moved to her ass, and he stood up, thrusting into her with unrelenting strokes.

She was helpless to his delicious assault and held on, absorbing every sensation, every tiny spark that still held life until she was caught up in the wave again, barreling toward the shore. He thrust one final time, and they came crashing down together in sweet bliss.

He went to let her down, but she tightened her arms around his neck afraid to let go, never wanting this moment to end.

She didn't have a plan for what came next and that scared her. But what scared her more was the thought of their future being the end of them.

Chapter 20

Sarah couldn't sleep. Not when she had so many things weighing so heavily on her mind. She wanted to tell Cooper, like a Band-Aid just rip it off and don't prolong it, but every time she tried, she couldn't find the words. She couldn't seem to get her head and her heart on the same page. So she let him fall asleep without a single mention that she was carrying his child.

She stared down at him, all gorgeous tan and long lashes and wondered what their baby would look like. If it would be a boy or girl. Would she have his blue eyes or her brown ones? Would the baby have freckles like Tommy? So many questions, and the more she thought about them the least scared she became.

She was being ridiculous. She needed to just tell Cooper and get it over with. If she didn't, the worrying would drive her insane. When he woke up she would tell him.

She was about to try to force herself to sleep when she heard a phone buzzing. She got up and found hers but there were no new notifications. She heard the buzzing again and found Cooper's phone in his pocket.

Not one to snoop, she was about to place it on the nightstand when the new text caught her eyes.

Just ordered my pack. September can't get here soon enough.

September? Even though it was against everything she believed in she opened the text. The name Gray was at the top and her eyes skimmed over the messages.

I have it all mapped out.

Can you just see our name in the headlines? Two shitheads walk the entire length of the Great Wall.

The Great Wall? He was going to China? Sarah's heart plummeted as her knees gave out, and she sat down on the edge of the bed, staring at the rest of the texts.

Hey, my man. The Great Wall. This September. You in?

Not sure yet. When do you need an answer by?

Don't skip out on me now! Leaving second week in September with or without you.

I'll let you know.

Tick Tock

It's going to be epic. I'll see you in September.

Her mouth dropped open, and all she could do was stare. Here she was, hoping that they had a future together, afraid to tell him about the baby because she was afraid it might scare him off. She was too stupid to realize that he was already planning to bail.

It was like her life was on repeat. She was about to be a single mother for the second time, and there was nothing she could do to fix it. Cooper already went ahead and made plans. Already was planning to be gone for… She scrolled back through the texts. Eighteen months. *Eighteen months!*

Sadness turned into anger as Cooper shifted beside her. Her hand landed on his shoulder and she shook him.

His eyes popped open, and she ignored how sexy he looked with droopy eyes and bedhead.

"What's wrong baby?"

"Don't you baby me!" she said, throwing his phone at him.

His reflexes were slow and the phone smacked him hard against the chest. "What the hell is wrong with you?"

"Wrong with *me*?" she said, a sinister laugh bubbling to the surface. "When were you going to tell me, huh? When?"

Her voice was getting louder, on the verge of screaming.

"Did you have a dream that you thought was real?" he asked, sitting up and rubbing the sleep from his eyes. "Because I'm fucking lost."

"China! When were you going to tell me you were going to China? For eighteen months? Are you kidding me! I get that you have a career. I knew that you would have to leave eventually, but I didn't think you'd be gone for eighteen fucking months. And maybe I'm the idiot for thinking this was more than it actually was, but forget about me. What about Tommy? For crying out loud he called you his father."

Thinking of Tommy and the disappointment that he would endure made her tear up. Her lip quivered as the pesky tears forced their way over her lids.

"Are you done?" he asked, standing up and walking toward her.

"Am I done?" He had some nerve. He was getting ready to up and leave her like she was yesterday's wash, and he had the audacity to ask her if she was done. "No, I'm not done! You made me trust you. You made me love you and now you're just going to walk away from me. From us." She walked away and grabbed the door. She pointed her finger to the hallway. "I think you should leave."

"Shut the damn door, I'm not leaving."

"Cooper, please. Don't make this any harder than it has to be."

She could have the baby and raise it on her own. She had done it before. She didn't need a man to help her. She was more than capable of handling things on her own. He didn't even need to know. Well, he would. His family practically made up the town, and she wouldn't be able to hide it for long. But she didn't have to tell him. Not yet. He could go off on his stupid trip, and she could stay back and raise their baby.

He didn't move, standing there in his boxer briefs and looking too damn desirable. She couldn't be strong with him there. She needed him to leave. She picked up his shoe and threw it at him. "I said get out!"

His reflexes most have kicked in because he caught the shoe before it hit him in the face. She picked up his jeans and tossed them, too. "I said get out."

He caught everything she threw at him then dropped the pile on the bed out of her reach. "What part of 'I'm not leaving' are you not hearing?"

"I don't want you here."

"If you stop yelling for two seconds I'll explain."

"I don't want to hear it. I just want you to go." She tried so hard to hold back the emotions, she wasn't a crier dammit, but the dam broke and tears flooded her cheeks. Uncontrollable sobs racked her body and she let her head fall into her hands.

Warm gentle hands wrapped around her and pulled her close. She wanted to push him away, to fight against his comfort because he was leaving anyway, but she wasn't strong enough to let go. She cried against his check, savoring the soft strokes of his fingers on her back.

"Hey," he said, as he took her chin in his hand and urged her to look at him.

She hated how much she loved those big beautiful eyes. How even though he betrayed her she could still lose herself in their depths. "I don't hate you," she said. "I'm just going to miss you."

"I'm not going to China."

"But… I saw the texts."

"I told Gray no. I told him that I had something better than walking the entire length of the Great Wall. I told him I found my soulmate, and there was nothing in the world that would take her away from me. Not even China."

Confused and unsure of his words Sarah tried to make sense of everything. "But the texts…"

"Gray doesn't take rejection very easily. He's convinced if he talks to me like I'm going I'll actually go, but baby, I told you, I'm not leaving you, and it hurts that you think I would."

"I didn't know what to think. And you never told me about it. I thought you were hiding it from me."

"I wouldn't hide it from you, and I was going to tell you, but every time I wanted to something came up or you seduced me," he said with that sexy smirk. "I'll never keep anything from you. I promise."

Her eyes dropped to the floor and he tilted her chin back to him.

"Now tell me." He ran a thumb under her eyes, catching the tears and wiping them away. "What is going on with you?"

He knew her better than anyone. He knew when something was weighing on her mind or when she was having a rough day. He knew how to make her happy and just the right things to say. Nobody ever knew her that well and maybe it was because she never let anyone else in but she wouldn't let Cooper in either, and he still managed to worm his way in.

"Talk to me. Why are you crying?"

She looked up into his eyes and took a deep breath, hoping for the best but preparing for the worst. "I'm pregnant."

Chapter 21

The declaration was like a smack across the face sending him spiraling into reality. *Pregnant?* How was that even possible? She was on the pill and most of the time he'd worn a condom.

"Are you sure?" he asked and instantly regretted the words as soon as they came out of his mouth.

Her eyes widened like he physically slapped her, and she stepped out of his embrace. He remembered the conversation they had about when she told Tommy's biological father about the pregnancy and how he'd reacted.

"I didn't mean that," he said, taking her back into his arms, hoping he could repair the damage before it was too late.

She shoved against him. "I knew you wouldn't be happy."

"It's not that I'm not happy. I'm just surprised. Weren't you?"

"Yes!" she cried. "I never meant for this to happen. And I understand if you don't want this. You didn't sign up for it, and I get it. I've raised a baby on my own before, and I can do it again so don't feel obligated to stick around."

He couldn't believe what she was saying, but he knew it wasn't her speaking; it was her fear. She had already assumed he'd walk away from her, and it annoyed him that she didn't give him more credit.

Her flipping out over the texts made perfect sense now. She was just waiting for him to do what he does best. She was waiting for him to ditch her. Well, she had another thing coming because that was the last damn thing he wanted to do. Baby or not he was in this for the long run.

"Stop trying to make me leave," he said.

"I just don't want you to feel trapped or like you have to stay. I want you to do what makes you happy."

He walked to her, taking her back in his arms and resting his forehead against hers. "Baby, don't you get it? You make me happy."

"But we didn't plan a baby."

"One thing I learned in all my travels—some of the best things are the things you don't plan for."

"You're not mad at me?"

"Why the hell would I be mad at you?"

"I didn't know antibiotics can counteract the pill. If I did I would've made sure…"

"Shh," he said, resting a finger on her lips. "No one is to blame here, especially not you."

"I'm scared," she admitted.

A smile tipped his lips. "I'm not."

Her eyebrows knitted together as she looked up at him. "You aren't?"

He shook his head. "I'm excited."

"Seriously?"

He loved the look of shock on her face. He kissed her nose and then her forehead.

"I always get excited before a new adventure, and I have a feeling this is going to be the best one yet."

***

"Mom, do you think it's a boy or a girl?" Tommy asked as they were driving to Sunday night dinner. They had just shared the news with him before leaving the house, afraid he wouldn't be able to keep the secret for too long.

Sarah shrugged. "I don't know. As long as she or he is healthy, I'll be happy."

Cooper turned to her, and even though she couldn't see his blue eyes behind his aviator sunglasses she knew they were filled with warmth and love. He rested his hand on her stomach that was only just starting to show and smiled.

Cooper gave a quick glance over his shoulder. "What do you hope it is, buddy?"

"A girl."

"What?" Sarah and Cooper both exclaimed.

"Then she won't play with my toys."

Sarah let out a laugh but not nearly as loud as Cooper's.

"Trust me, girl or boy you're not getting out of sharing your toys. My sisters stole mine all the time."

"Man!" Tommy crossed his arms and slouched into the seat.

Cooper pulled up to his parents' farmhouse and put the car in park. He glanced up at the house then back to Tommy. "But don't worry. I have a feeling you'll have plenty of toys and sharing won't be a problem."

Tommy's face lit up, and Sarah cut Cooper a look. "Don't go promising him these things," she said, still having to remind Cooper that seven-year-old boy's minds were like steel traps. Once you insinuated something they held you to it, just like the dog scenario that Tommy was still begging for. She hadn't caved yet, but she knew it was only a matter of time before she did or Cooper just came home with a newly adopted puppy. She definitely wouldn't put it past him, and that was okay because his impulsiveness was one of the things she loved about him.

"With my family, I think that's a promise I can keep."

Sarah imagined Tommy and the new generation of Hayes children running around the open field, cousins by blood and friends by choice, getting dirty and getting into trouble. Cooper would join the fun and teach them how to climb trees while she watched from the porch with his sisters.

It was a welcoming sight and so far from anything she had ever imagined before Cooper had come into her life. He was a major curveball that made her forget about her plans and act on instinct. Made her realize that the best things in life can't be planned.

"What are you three still doing out here?" Betty Hayes called from the front porch, waving her hands for them to come to her already.

Sarah rested her hand on top of her stomach, smiling down at the new life growing inside her then up at her two favorite boys. "You ready to do this?" she asked.

"Oh yeah," Cooper said. "Once Grandma finds out you're pregnant, I'll be the golden child again."

Sarah laughed. "Was that your evil plan this whole time?"

He gave her that adorable smirk that made her insides melt. "You know it."

He leaned across his seat, cupping her cheek and pressing a long, loving kiss to her lips.

"Ew. Come on," Tommy whined from the backseat. "I'm out of here." He opened the car and jumped out, greeting Betty at the top of the stairs just as Carol and Jonathon Hayes stepped out.

Tears filled Sarah's eyes—damn pregnancy hormones— as she watched Tommy get engulfed by people who already treated him like their own, who had accepted her and her son with open arms.

Cooper kissed beneath her eyelids. "Don't cry, baby."

"They're happy tears. Nothing to be alarmed about."

"After you started crying over a puppy video the other day, not much alarms me."

"It was so cute," she said with a laugh and felt the tears welling up again.

He rested his forehead on hers, running his thumbs beneath her lids. "Man, I love you."

"Why? I'm an emotional mess who is about to blow up like a blimp."

"You're a beautiful mess. My beautiful mess and you're not going to blow up like a blimp just a balloon. Like the big one's at the Thanksgiving Day Parade. Maybe we'll tie a string to you and…"

She smacked his chest. "Stop talking or I will hurt you."

With a laugh, he wrapped his arms around her. She loved how he could lighten a mood up so easily and make her laugh effortlessly. For so long, she took everything seriously, too seriously, and Cooper brought out the carefree girl who was hiding inside of her.

"Do we have to go inside," he asked as he trailed a finger down the length of her neck, sending goosebumps exploding across her body.

"Yes," she breathed.

"Why don't we leave Tommy with my family for a few minutes, and I'll take you back home and show you all the dirty thoughts I've been having since you walked out in this dress this morning."

"Only a few minutes?" she asked with a raised eyebrow.

He cupped her cheek, and she nuzzled into the warmth of his hand.

"Baby, with the thoughts I've been having, I'd be lucky to last a minute."

She kissed his cheek then leaned close to his ear. "With all the thoughts I've been having, I'd need longer than a minute."

He hissed through his teeth, and she nipped at his earlobe before pulling away. "Too bad I'm hungry," she said and jumped out of the car before he could grab her.

"You're evil!" he yelled as she walked away with a huge smile on her face.

She greeted everyone as she made her way up the porch steps and was instantly embraced.

"My grandson behaving himself?" Betty asked.

Sarah turned to the car where Cooper still hadn't exited, probably waiting for things to settle. "What do you think?"

"That's my boy!" she said, throwing Cooper a thumbs up.

"Oh, good you're here," Kate said, hooking her arm through Sarah's and pulling her inside, a glass of red wine in her hand. "I need a buffer."

"For what?"

"Who do you think? My insufferable grandmother who would probably artificially inseminate me if she could." Kate took a generous sip of her wine and Sarah bit back a laugh.

She patted Kate's hand. "Don't worry, I have you covered."

"Unless you're pregnant there's no…" Kate turned to Sarah, eyes wide, mouth dropping in a perfect O. "Oh my god. Are you…?"

Sarah lifted her finger to her lips then nodded.

"Holy shit."

Sarah hushed her. "You're the first person I've told

other than my parents." They took a trip to Connecticut last weekend for Cooper to meet her parents and of course, like with everyone, he won them over almost as soon as he walked in the door. "We're going to announce it at dinner."

Kate grabbed her and yanked her against her chest. "I'm so happy."

"Me too," Sarah said.

"Cooper as a dad. Oh man, if his kid turns out anything like him you're in for some trouble."

Cooper walked in the door then, looking devilishly handsome with his signature smirk as he joined his brothers, Caleb, and Sam. "Don't I know it."

"What are you guys talking about?" Hadley asked as she approached, Lady at her feet.

Kate tilted her head toward Sarah. "Sarah's pregnant."

"What?" Hadley exclaimed, and Sarah shot Kate a look.

Kate held her hands up. "Sorry! I'm just so excited and Hads and I come as a unit. You can't tell one without telling the other."

"Okay, just don't tell anyone else."

"My lips are sealed," Kate said as Hadley took Sarah in a hug.

"What'd I miss?" Shay asked, approaching with a growing Matthew in her arms.

"Sarah's pregnant," Hadley said.

Shay's mouth dropped. "What?"

"You guys are the worst!" Sarah said with a laugh.

"Sorry." Hadley shrugged. "But that unit Kate was talking about includes Shay. Cassie, too, but she's currently cornered by Grandma, and now it includes you, too."

Those damn pregnancy tears started to press at the back of her eyes. "Really?"

"Hell yeah," Kate said. "We girls have to stick together. Plus, it helps that you're practically famous now and that's one step closer to me meeting Leonardo DiCaprio."

Everyone laughed.

"This girl used to have her entire bedroom wall covered with his face. I swear I felt like I was being watched every time I went in there," Hadley said.

"It's not my fault your crush wasn't a celebrity. I bet if he was, his mug would've been all over the walls."

Sarah was about to ask who Hadley's crush was when she saw the look Hadley shot Kate. Clearly, it was something she didn't want to discuss. Hadley's eyes quickly darted to Sam. If Sarah had blinked she would have missed it, but in that flash of a moment Sarah's question was answered.

"Dinner's ready," Carol Hayes announced.

They all took their seats, and once the first course was finished, Cooper took Sarah's hand under the table. He gave it a squeeze and she turned to him with a nod.

"Ready?" she asked.

"You know I was born ready."

"You did not just say that."

"I did and better yet, it totally turned you on."

"Okay, Casanova, focus."

Cooper cleared his throat. "I…We have something we'd like to share," Cooper said, getting the entire family's attention. All eyes turned to them and without even taking a breath Cooper blurted, "Sarah's pregnant. We're going to have a baby."

Betty dropped her fork, a loud clang slashing through the excited reactions, and everyone turned to look at her. Her hands covered her mouth and pure joy radiated off her face as her bright blue eyes landed on Sarah. "He knocked you up?" she asked.

Sarah laughed and nodded. "He did."

"Cooper, I'm so proud of you!" Betty jumped up from her seat, dancing on her toes as she came at them with open arms, declaring Cooper the golden child... for now.

The End

Thank you for reading! I hope you loved Cooper and Sarah as much as I did.
Please consider leaving a review.

Hung up on Hadley Coming October 2017

~Keep Reading for an excerpt from Moments with Mason~

Chapter 1

Mason Hayes stepped back and looked around the refurbished barn that was now the tasting room for his very own brewery. From that first batch, he made at twenty-two in his parents' basement, he never would've imagined that beer-making would become his lifelong passion or that he'd be a business owner at the age of twenty-seven.

"You did it." His best friend and brother, Cooper smacked him on the back.

"*We* did it," he said, giving credit where credit was due. Cooper, who hadn't stayed put in one place for more than a couple of weeks since he graduated high school, had stayed in Red Maple Falls for four months to help Mason get things running.

Mason never would have gotten everything done in time for his opening in a couple weeks. None of this would've been possible without the help of his five siblings, his parents, and most definitely not without the generous loan his grandparents had given him.

It was a dream come true made possible by the people he loved most, even if they all were a big pain in his ass.

"I need to head out and see if Dad needs help with anything on the farm before the bulk of the storm hits. That way the festival can start right back up when the weather clears."

The Fall festival at their parent's farm happened every

year from the end of September to the end of October that required all Hayes' hands on deck. Mason had felt guilty about not being around as much he usually was.

"Let me know if you need help," he offered.

Cooper's blue eyes travelled around the tasting room. "If you haven't noticed, you have a brewery to open."

"Bad timing on my part."

"The festival happens every year. This is a once in a lifetime. We can manage. Besides, I'm here what else can Mom and Dad possibly need?"

"Peace and quiet."

"Whatever. They love having me around."

"That's because I gave them earplugs."

"Funny."

"Are Grandma and Grandpa down at the farm too?"

"No, Mom told them to stay home today. Which reminds me I forgot Mom asked me to check on them to see if they needed anything, so they don't try to wander out in the storm."

"Because that would stop them," Mason said. He loved his grandparents fiercely, respected them, owed them his life for believing in him enough to loan him such a huge chunk of money, but Betty and Harold Hayes were stubborn as all hell and getting progressively worse with age. If they wanted to go out, Cooper stopping by and offering to do it for them wouldn't deter them.

"That's what I said. Mom was still adamant about it. Ever since the old man's stint in the hospital, Mom's been on edge."

While their grandfather was recovered and back to his normal obstinate eighty-two-year-old self after a bout with heat stroke, Mason understood their mother's concern.

Sitting in that hospital waiting room, not knowing what the hell was going on and unable to get answers was torture. Mason had never felt so helpless in his entire life. Even he'd been making extra trips to his grandparents' house since that dreadful day, finding ridiculous excuses to stop by and check in on them.

"Hopefully, I can be in and out before Grandma corners me and tries to set me up with one of her friend's grandkids. I don't know how many times I can tell her I'm not interested."

Mason laughed. Betty Hayes was desperate for grandkids and had taken matters into her own hands by offering up any single girl she could sink her work worn hands into. They had thought when their oldest brother Matt had knocked up his new bride they'd get a bit of a break, but if anything, Betty Hayes was more relentless than ever.

"I don't think she'll stop until we're all married off with kids."

"She can keep it up, but it'll never happen. Me with kids?" Cooper scoffed. "Now that is the biggest joke of all."

"Especially since you're still a kid yourself."

Cooper grabbed Mason's hand and smacked him upside the head before Mason could scramble out of the way.

"What the hell was that for?" Mason asked, knowing damn well his brothers didn't need a reason to hit him. It's something they'd done since they were kids.

"Trying to knock some sense into you."

"If that's the case you should be hitting yourself."

"I think I'm the sanest person in this family."

"And I think you just found you're calling."

"Calling for what?"

"Standup comedian, because that shit is hilarious."

Cooper shook his head, but before he could retort, Mason patted his back. "Need to work on your comebacks though. Come on, I'll follow you out."

Mason hadn't eaten all day and needed a lunch break if he was ever going to get through the rest of the night.

"Damn, it's coming down in buckets," Cooper said as he opened the door, letting the sound of rushing water echo through the space. "I'll catch you later." He pulled the collar of his shirt up and dashed toward their dad's old beater.

Mason pulled the hood of his sweatshirt over his head and jogged to his truck, being careful not to land in any deep puddles. Cooper beeped as he drove away, and Mason offered a nod though he doubted his brother could see him through the sheet of rain.

Mason turned his Bronco onto the main road, his windshield wipers working overtime to try and clear the rain. It was one hell of a storm blowing through, and he worried his parking lot would turn into a mud pit. He opted against putting down blacktop because he wanted to keep the rustic feel—plus, he didn't want to add to his overhead costs.

Now he was questioning that decision. He'd been doing that a lot lately—double guessing every decision he had made, wondering if what he decided now would bite him in the ass down the line. He wanted to be a success, but more than anything he wanted to prove to himself that he could do this. That he could take the intelligence he was known for and create it into something he was passionate about.

He leaned forward to get a better view of the road and tried to ignore that annoying voice in the back of his mind when he spotted a figure walking down the side of the street. He didn't recognize the person from behind, but that didn't stop him from slowing down.

Born and raised in Red Maple Falls, Mason knew everyone and would never let a neighbor fend for themselves in this type of weather. He pulled his truck to the side of the road and rolled down his window.

On closer inspection, he could see the petite, soft curves of a female. She kept her head down, hiding her face behind a curtain of long and wavy, reddish brown hair that was sopping wet as she continued to walk on by without offering as much as a glance in his direction. Concerned for her well-being, Mason put the truck back in drive and rolled alongside of her.

"Can I give you a ride?" he called out, trying to make his voice heard over the relentless wind and loud smacking rain drops.

"I'm good," she said, but he detected a hint of sadness in her voice. Her shoulders were raised, body hunched probably trying to keep water from running down her neck. She wouldn't look at him so he had no idea if he knew who she was, but regardless if he knew her or not, he couldn't just leave her out in this monsoon.

He put his truck in park and jumped out. He came to a stop in front of the girl, who paused, her eyes wide and startled before she tried to step around him.

"Hey," he said, reaching his hand out to her shoulder, but she flinched at his gesture, causing him to retract his hand. "I'm sorry. I didn't mean to scare you. I just want to give you a ride." He removed his hood, so she could see his face, hoping that would give her a little peace of mind.

She finally looked up; her golden-brown eyes reminded him of a fresh poured amber ale, making him momentarily forget how to speak. He definitely didn't know her; he would have recognized those eyes anywhere.

Big rain drops ran down Mason's face and neck, pooling where his hoodie met his skin. "Please," he said. "You're soaked through, and you're shivering. Let me give you a ride."

"I'm sorry, but I don't trust strangers."

"Then allow me to introduce myself. I'm Mason Hayes." He held out his hand, but she only looked at it, so he let it fall back to his side. She was hesitant and she was scared, and that was the last thing he wanted, so he broke out the signature Hayes smile known to charm anyone it came in contact with. "If that doesn't mean anything to you then that tells me you're not from around here."

"Are you famous or something?"

"In our own right," he said with a laugh. "I was born and raised in this town. My parents own Basil Hill Farms that's currently running the state's famous Fall Festival, my sister owns Serenity Glass Blowing Studios, my sister-in-law owns Sweet Dream Bakery, my soon to be brother-in-law owns the Chain and Spoke. Oh, and my oldest brother is the Sheriff, so I really can't be a serial killer because that would be bad for business. So please, let me give you a ride."

She stood there, rain sluicing down her black leather coat as she fidgeted with her hands. Finally, with a deep breath she nodded. "All right."

Thank god, he thought as he ran over to the passenger door and opened it. She slid a backpack off her shoulder, and he reached out to take it for her, but she aggressively hugged the bag to her chest.

"I just wanted to help," he said. "I'm sorry."

"I got it," she answered, tossing the bag up on the seat.

She looked up at the truck and placed her foot on the running board. It was still a bit of a climb for her, so he held his hand out to help her. "I don't bite," he said.

She hesitated for a moment before slipping her hand into his. It was small and delicate, but he imagined the girl it was attached to was the total opposite. She used his hand as leverage as she hoisted her petite frame into the large truck.

Once she was settled he shut the door and ran back to the driver's side.

Her small frame shook as she blew into her hands. Raised in the White Mountains, Mason was used to cold weather, but he could tell his passenger wasn't. He reached behind him, grabbing a thick blanket he kept in his truck and draped it over her shoulders. "That should help," he said. She looked at him, shock widening her eyes, lips parting ever so slightly. She yanked on the edges of the blanket, pulling it tighter around her body.

He reached over to the dials and turned the heat on full blast.

"Thanks," she said as the stiffness began to leave her body, and she sank a little farther into the seat.

He pulled the truck back onto the road and headed in the direction she had been walking. "Where to?"

She pointed a long slim finger straight. Her nails weren't painted, but kept short and clean. She didn't have a ring so she wasn't married. "Make a left at the end of the road and then take it all the way down."

Mason's eyebrow arched in curiosity as he glanced over at her. The only thing at the end of Turtle Creek Road was the campsite. "You're staying at Turtle Creek Reserve?"

She nodded.

Mason was the quiet one in his family, never wanting to compete with five siblings, so he only spoke when he had something important to say or to rip on one of his brothers or sisters. Being part of such a large family, he never had to work for a response, at least not in a way she was making him.

"What's your name by the way?" he asked, realizing she never told him. Just because he didn't know who she was didn't mean he had never heard of her.

"Why?"

"It would be nice to have a name to go with your face. Know who I'm talking to."

She fidgeted with the strap on her backpack instead of speaking.

"Or I can just call you rain girl. Aquawoman. Kathy Seldon though it was really Don Lockwood who was singin' in the rain."

"Cassie," she mumbled just loud enough for him to hear.

"She speaks," he said. "So, Cassie." He liked the way her name rolled off his tongue. "What were you doing walking out in this storm? Planning on singing and dancing?"

"No."

He turned a glance in her direction, waiting for her to elaborate.

Her lips parted and trembled as a tear fell down her cheek, causing Mason to shift uncomfortably in his seat. Even with three sisters he never got used to a girl crying. It made him feel helpless, and there was nothing he hated more.

She angrily swiped at the teardrop as if she couldn't believe she let it fall in the first place. "If you most know, I was hoping to find a job, but it seems like no one is hiring. So now I have no idea what I'm going to do." She laughed, but it wasn't a humorous sort of laugh it sounded more deranged. "I should've known better. Things never work out for me. Did I honestly think a miracle would happen? Miracles aren't even real. They're just made up lies people talk about to give you false hope."

She continued to vent, and Mason sat there listening to everything she was saying. It's what he did. The reason his brothers and sisters came to him whenever they were having a problem was because he was a good listener. Most of the time they would work their problems out themselves before he could even get a word in.

"I'm sorry," she finally said, a slight tinge of crimson filling her cheeks before she shook her head. "I didn't mean to dump on you. It's been a crappy day."

Mason pulled the truck to a stop, and Cassie let out a sigh. "I understand," she said. "I wouldn't want to be stuck in a car with a lunatic either." She began to remove the blanket and pull her bag onto her shoulder when he cut the wheel and headed back in the opposite direction.

"What are you doing?" she asked, and he didn't like the panic lacing her tone, so he turned that Hayes charm on again.

"You need a job."

"Yes, I do, but—"

"We're going to see about getting you a job."

"I told you, no one is hiring. I've been everywhere."

"You haven't been everywhere."

"But I walked up and down Main Street."

"This place isn't on Main Street."

"I don't have a car. I can't walk far."

"This place is closer than Main Street."

"How is that possible?"

With a slight smile still on his face, Mason said,

"Miracles," before he turned his truck into the parking lot of Five Leaf Brewery and shifted into park.

"I didn't even know this place was here," Cassie said, staring at the front of the refurbished barn.

"It's new. What do you know about beer?" Secretly he hoped she had some knowledge, but even if she didn't she could learn.

"Actually, a lot. I waitressed at a sports bar with over forty taps of craft beer."

"Perfect." He needed to hire someone to work the tasting room. He planned on waiting a while, taking his family up on their offer to volunteer their time while he saved some money, but Cassie desperately needed a job, and he wouldn't be able to sleep if he dropped her off at the campsite and never looked back. The fact that she had knowledge about beer already was somewhat of a miracle. "Now come on."

"Where?"

"You have an interview."

"What? No. I look horrible." She tried running fingers through her hair, but kept getting snagged on knots.

Mason glanced over at her, her hair was sopping wet, hanging in long waves on her shoulders, and her eyes were a little puffy around the edges, but he could see beyond the disheveled mess and see the beauty beneath. "I have a feeling that's impossible."

Mason hopped out of the truck and was happy when Cassie was right behind him. He stuck the key into the lock. "You work here?" she asked, sounding a bit surprised.

"Something like that."

"Do you think the owner will like me?"

"I think the owner will like you just fine."

He held the door, letting her in from the rain. She had grabbed her backpack and hoisted it up on her shoulder as she looked around the tasting room. Drops of water dripped from her jacket onto the floor he still needed to mop.

"Wow. This place is great. Look at the craftsmanship of these tables and benches."

"Earl does great work. He runs Red Maple Falls Wood Studios."

She dragged her finger across a tabletop as she walked toward the bar. "Five Leaf Brewery," she said. "I like it."

"Thanks."

"What does it mean?"

"I have two brothers and three sisters. The five points make the leaf whole." He shrugged. "I wouldn't be who I am today without them."

"That's really sweet." Realization settled on her face. "Wait. *You* own this place?"

He crossed his arms over his chest and leaned against the bar, a sense of pride swelling inside of him. "I do." It was hard not to keep the smile off his face as he looked around at all that he had accomplished.

"Why didn't you just interview me in the truck then?" Cassie asked, shrugging out of her dripping wet leather jacket and hanging it on a chair. He reached for a rag behind the bar and handed it to her to wipe her jacket dry. She took the rag without hesitation and pulled it down each sleeve then peered back up at him, her eyebrows pulling tight above the bridge of her nose. "Why bring me back here?"

"I wanted to get you out of the rain."

"Afraid I was going to melt?" she said with a laugh, and it surprised him how much he liked the sound. It was light and sweet, and he had a feeling it wasn't something she let flow freely too often.

"I was raised to help those in need."

Her body stiffened, her golden eyes darkened like a storm was brewing within her and not just outside. "I'm not a charity case."

"Never said you were."

"I didn't need your help, you know."

Her sudden defense mode made him curious. Anybody else would have brushed the comment off, possibly even admired his chivalrous side. Though, he had always been good at reading people, and he could tell that she wasn't just anybody. He wanted to know who the girl beneath the leather coat and golden eyes really was.

His lip quirked at the corner when he replied, "A simple thank you would suffice."

Acknowledgements

Cassie Mae, an acknowledgement at the back of the book seems like it's not enough to tell you how grateful I am for you. Just know that none of this would be possible if it wasn't for you. You talk me up when I'm down, talk me down when I'm overwhelmed and somehow always know when I need a phone call. And all of that aside, I couldn't ask for a better editor. You ask the hard questions that make me think and cut back on my repetitiveness. Thank you!

Mom! Another book down and another book that you helped create. From your keen eye to your vivid imagination you breathe life into all of my stories. Thanks for being my best friend and more importantly an amazing beta reader.

Eric, it's funny because I know you don't read these but I still feel it necessary to include you. Truth be told, I couldn't do what I do without your constant support and unwavering love. Thanks for dealing with my crazy!

My Beta girls, thank you for always being there to cheer me on, help me out with random questions, your priceless advice and your support. I couldn't ask for a better group of girls to have by my side on this wild journey.

Jackson, my seven-year-old guru who helped me get Tommy's voice spot on. Thanks, little guy!

Amanda Walker, my amazingly talented cover designer, thank you for bringing my visions to life. This cover is so perfect!

To my readers, from the bottom of my heart, thank you. You're the reason I get to do what I love and for that I will be forever grateful.

About the Author

Theresa Paolo lives on Long Island, NY with her fiancé and their fish. She is the author of NA and Adult contemporary romances. Her debut novel (NEVER) AGAIN, released in Fall 2013 with Berkley (Penguin) and the companion novel (ONCE) AGAIN released Summer 2014. Mad About Matt, the first book in her new Red Maple Falls series, released March 2017.

She put her love of writing on hold while she received her Bachelor's Degree in Marketing. When she's not writing, she's reading, brewery hopping, daydreaming, wasting time on Pinterest, or can be found chatting away on Twitter and Facebook. She also writes YA romance under Tessa Marie.

Made in the USA
Middletown, DE
02 October 2017